Jessie reacted, breaking into a run as she wove through the trees, her hair streaming out behind her, her eyes on the dark creek ahead. She felt a hand on her shoulder, and then the weight of the man on her back, and she fell, scratching and clawing, twisting around to fight back.

The Apache had caught her, but it was like catching a bobcat bare-handed. Forked, stiffened fingers were driven into the Indian's eyes and he howled with pain, covering his face as Jessica drove her knee up into his groin.

She rolled away from underneath him and stood panting, facing him. The Apache, the grin gone now, his eyes bloody, leaped for her. He caught a side-kick to the face for his trouble. Deciding enough was enough, he drew his rawhide-handled knife.

Also in the LONE STAR series
from Jove

LONGARM AND THE LONE STAR
    LEGEND
LONGARM AND THE LONE STAR
    VENGEANCE
LONGARM AND THE LONE STAR
    BOUNTY
LONE STAR AND THE STOCKYARD
    SHOWDOWN
LONE STAR AND THE RIVERBOAT
    GAMBLERS
LONE STAR AND THE MESCALERO
    OUTLAWS
LONE STAR AND THE AMARILLO
    RIFLES
LONE STAR AND THE SCHOOL
    FOR OUTLAWS
LONE STAR ON THE TREASURE
    RIVER
LONE STAR AND THE MOON
    TRAIL FEUD
LONE STAR AND THE GOLDEN
    MESA
LONGARM AND THE LONE STAR
    RESCUE
LONE STAR AND THE RIO GRANDE
    BANDITS
LONE STAR AND THE BUFFALO
    HUNTERS
LONE STAR AND THE BIGGEST
    GUN IN THE WEST
LONE STAR AND THE APACHE
    WARRIOR
LONE STAR AND THE GOLD MINE
    WAR
LONE STAR AND THE CALIFORNIA
    OIL WAR
LONE STAR AND THE ALASKAN
    GUNS
LONE STAR AND THE WHITE
    RIVER CURSE
LONGARM AND THE LONE STAR
    DELIVERANCE

LONE STAR AND THE TOMBSTONE
    GAMBLE
LONE STAR AND THE
    TIMBERLAND TERROR
LONE STAR IN THE CHEROKEE
    STRIP
LONE STAR AND THE OREGON
    RAIL SABOTAGE
LONE STAR AND THE MISSION
    WAR
LONE STAR AND THE GUNPOWDER
    CURE
LONGARM AND THE LONE STAR
    SHOWDOWN
LONE STAR AND THE LAND
    BARONS
LONE STAR AND THE GULF
    PIRATES
LONE STAR AND THE INDIAN
    REBELLION
LONE STAR AND THE NEVADA
    MUSTANGS
LONE STAR AND THE CON MAN'S
    RANSOM
LONE STAR AND THE
    STAGECOACH WAR
LONGARM AND THE LONE STAR
    MISSION
LONE STAR AND THE TWO GUN
    KID
LONE STAR AND THE SIERRA
    SWINDLERS
LONE STAR IN THE BIG HORN
    MOUNTAINS
LONE STAR AND THE DEATH
    TRAIN
LONE STAR AND THE RUSTLER'S
    AMBUSH
LONE STAR AND THE TONG'S
    REVENGE
LONE STAR AND THE SKY
    WARRIORS

WESLEY ELLIS

LONE STAR

AND THE SKY WARRIORS

JOVE BOOKS, NEW YORK

LONE STAR AND THE SKY WARRIORS

A Jove Book / published by arrangement with
the author

PRINTING HISTORY
Jove edition / September 1987

ISBN: 0-515-09170-7

Jove Books are published by The Berkley Publishing Group,
200 Madison Avenue, New York, New York 10016.
The name "JOVE" and the "J" logo
are trademarks belonging to Jove Publications, Inc.

PRINTED IN THE UNITED STATES OF AMERICA

10 9 8 7 6 5 4 3 2 1

Chapter 1

The crimson smear covered half of the grassy valley. It made Ki think of a battlefield where a giant had been slain. The body had been dragged away but the gore remained.

"It's big enough," was his comment.

The honey blonde with the sea-green eyes glanced at the man beside her. She too was fascinated by the hundreds—or was it thousands?—of yards of crimson silk draped over the earth.

"Sperry claims it's the largest ever attempted," Jessica Starbuck replied, brushing away a stray lock of wind-drifted hair from her face.

The two sat in their rented buggy on this hill above San Francisco: the breathtakingly beautiful daughter of a million-aire and her half-Japanese, half-American bodyguard and friend. Below them antlike figures scurried around the great silk form spilled out across the meadow.

"I thought I'd seen everything," Ki said. "When you told me about Horace Sperry and his hot-air balloon I thought I knew what to expect. But that— Is he mad?"

"Father used to call him eccentric," Jessica said, with a soft smile that parted her lips. "And a dreamer. But then dreamers have a way of making things happen sometimes."

It was hard for either of them to believe much could come of this particular dream.

Both Ki and Jessica knew about the Frenchmen, the Mont-golfier brothers, who had first flown in 1783, and both were aware of the observation balloons used during the Civil War on both sides. But Horace Sperry envisioned a new world, a

1

country criss-crossed by hot air balloons, some carrying cargo, others up to fifty passengers.

It was a wild notion, but who knew? Someone had taken Sperry's dream seriously—enough to try to kill him and destroy his balloon. That was where Jessica and Ki had entered the picture.

"We'd better go on down and talk to the man," Ki said, turning toward the buggy. "Have you seen him before?"

"I met him. Once. On the ranch. He had come to ask Father for some help for a current project." Jessica smiled again and shook her head. "He wanted to drill a hole to the center of the earth."

Ki shrugged. Anything, he supposed, was possible, but these schemes of Sperry's seemed to be on the very borderline of possibility. Maybe Horace Sperry was just a man ahead of his time.

They drove the buggy down into the long valley and approached the scarlet balloon. Men were working on the fabric with sailmakers' needles. Others were untangling lines. To the side was the gondola that went with the huge silk balloon. Made of wicker, it was the size of a miner's cabin.

Sperry, Ki decided, might be many things, but he certainly didn't think small.

Ki halted the buggy, and Sperry himself appeared from behind the gondola, calling something to an assistant, holding a piece of machinery in his hand.

The balding man with the huge white muttonchops approached the buggy and spoke to Jessica and Ki as if they had been there all along.

"The butterfly valve again... I think the coil spring is jamming on me. Water vapor. I shouldn't have used steel."

He continued peering at the workings of his burner for another long minute before he became aware of the need for courtesies.

"Jessica, I'm pleased you could make it. This whole thing is a rotten mess." He waved a hand vaguely toward his rotten mess.

Jessie stepped down from the buggy, removed her flat-crowned hat and walked to Sperry, taking his grimy hand.

2

"You've been having trouble besides mechanical ones."

"Yes. Saboteurs! Incredible. How could anyone think of interfering with scientific advancement?"

"There's usually a reason."

"Yes, but this— It's disgraceful," the scientist, genuinely offended, said.

"Do you know Ki?" Jessica asked. "Ki, this is Dr. Sperry. Horace, my good friend Ki."

Sperry blinked as if puzzled. His mind was still on the coil spring. "I don't think so. Ki?" Finally he put his hand out and Ki took it, suppressing a smile.

"Is there somewhere we can talk?" Jessie asked. "If Ki and I are to help we'll have to know a little more than your letter told us."

"I have a tent. Yes. The gondola is behind schedule too. I think Melinda is . . ."

And then Melinda Sperry put in her appearance. She was totally unlike any preconceptions Ki had held about the daughter of a scientist. Her hair was long, red and gold, trailing down her back. He breasts were full and high, her waist narrow, hips flaring boldly. Her smile was warm and generous, her blue eyes sparkling.

"I was just telling them about the gondola problem," Sperry said.

"Father, you haven't introduced us yet."

"What? Oh, this is Jessica Starbuck. Her friend . . ."

"Ki," Ki said, and he took the woman's surprisingly strong hand is his own.

"I wrote to Jessica, remember?" Horace Sperry asked.

"Yes, Father," Melinda answered.

"I've been explaining about the butterfly valve."

Melinda was still studying the tall, muscular Ki, her eyes alert and interested.

Jessica said, "We would like to sit down somewhere and get the entire story of what's happening here."

"Certainly. Father? Tea and cookies and conversation. You've left your guests standing here."

"Have I?" Sperry blinked again. "Sorry. This is very important, you see. Without the valve our burner won't be of

3

much use, will it? If Melinda says it's time for tea and cookies then it must be."

They followed the absent-minded scientist and his daughter to a patched and discolored army tent beyond the great gondola and ducked inside. A teakettle whistled on an iron stove. Books and scrawled notes, diagrams and wooden crates were scattered everywhere. Melinda cleared some of the mess off the plank table and invited Jessica and Ki to sit.

Finally persuaded to place his work aside, Sperry hunched forward on his folding wooden chair and explained what he was trying to do and why.

"There will be a ship from the Orient arriving in San Francisco on the twelfth, carrying overseas mail destined for a man in St. Louis. I intend to pick up this mail and deliver it to him via hot-air balloon."

"You're doing all of this to deliver someone's mail?" Jessie asked in disbelief.

"I am doing it, young lady, to prove it can be done. The sponsor of the expedition is doing it because he's tired of waiting months for his cargo and personal mail."

"It's Gustav Schultz," Melinda told them. Ki hadn't heard the name and said so. "He's a St. Louis brewer and a millionaire. He's offering a fifty-thousand-dollar prize to anyone who can prove the feasibility of air-cargo *and* bring him his mail."

"That's a lot of money," Ki said.

"To us it's an enormous sum, and we need it badly, but apparently it's nothing much to Gustav Schultz."

"What about the sabotage?" Jessica asked.

"That started immediately. Several crates were thrown into the bay, crates containing necessary parts. We've had lines cut, our balloon slashed, and once a shot was fired at us—though that may have been a hunter."

"Have you any idea who's behind it?"

"Gregor, maybe. Or McCarthy."

"Who are they?"

"Ascensionists. Fifty thousand dollars is a lot of money, Jessica. Father and I aren't the only ones willing to try for it."

"Amateurs," Dr. Sperry sniffed. "Fairground ascensionists. Men of no vision. I believe there are six other balloonists in the hunt."

4

"You don't have any evidence against these people, then?"

"No, it could have been any of them," Melinda said, "and I suppose it could be anyone else in San Francisco."

"Random vandalism?"

"Not exactly that," the redhead said. "You see there are a lot of wagers being made on the race. Every saloon in town has the odds chalked up behind the bar. If someone, say, had placed a large wager on McCarthy it would only make sense to eliminate the competition."

"Have any of the other balloonists had equipment damaged?" Ki asked.

"I don't know. Gregor's camp is like an army bivouac. You know, men with rifles standing guard. He won't talk to anybody."

"Except the press," her father put in.

"Oh, yes." Melinda laughed. "The newspapermen are everywhere. One of them even asked if he could ride with us."

"I don't think he was a newspaperman," Dr. Sperry said.

"Well, maybe he wasn't. At any rate we turned him down."

"Are the other balloons capable of carrying a gondola like yours?" Ki inquired.

"Of course not. Well, Gregor's may approach the capacity of my gondola, but most of the others are small-minded attempts. As I say, fairground types. They just can't see what we have the chance to accomplish here. All they see is dollar signs."

"Father's thought is that even if we fail to win the race we'll have added immeasurably to a new science: that of flight. True, we'll be so far in debt if we *don't* win that we may never be able to apply what we learn; but think of it, Ki: mail and supplies moving from the coasts to inland destinations, delivering food or medicine to inaccessible areas. No one has ever attempted to fly this far before, and if it is accomplished perhaps the eyes of industry and the government will finally be opened."

"It *will* be accomplished," Sperry said with conviction. "And we *will* win, if we can keep these vandals away. With the money, I shall prepare for my next project."

5

"And what is that, Dr. Sperry?" Jessica Starbuck asked.

"What? Why the moon, young lady! A balloon flight to the moon!"

Outside Jessica and Ki discussed things. Ki was still chuckling over the professor's last pronouncement. "You called him a dreamer—he's proving that to me, Jessie. The *moon!*"

"What about this, Ki?" she asked, nodding toward the deflated balloon. "You think any of them can reach St. Louis?"

"I know nothing about the art. There are half a dozen or so men who seem to think it possible."

"And some willing to stoop to sabotage."

"Yes." They walked in a slow circle around the great silk balloon. "All we can do for now is wait and be watchful. If—" An approaching surrey caused Ki's head to turn, his sentence to break off. A young man with a buckskin horse in the traces rolled into the camp at speed, waving a hand at Jessica and Ki. He wore light brown tweed and a white hat.

As he leaped from the surrey and walked toward them Ki saw that he was tall, broad-shouldered, fair-haired, and clean shaven, with clear blue eyes.

He started to speak, looked briefly puzzled, and then approached more slowly, his eyes finding Jessica Starbuck more than appealing. "Sorry," he said. "I assumed you were Melinda Sperry. You don't see many women in jeans around . . ." And not many who looked like this one, he thought but didn't say as he took a closer measure of Jessica Starbuck's beauty.

"Afraid not. I think she's in the tent."

The man didn't seem to be in a hurry to leave. "I'm Cadge Dana—*San Francisco Post.*"

"The man who wants to go along on this odyssey," Jessica said.

"That's right. Sure. It's a reporter's dream. I wanted another crack at the professor. My editor's given me permission and there's a news syndicate interested."

"Dr. Sperry doesn't like the idea very much."

"Maybe what I've got to tell him now will change his mind. The *Post*'s willing to put up five hundred dollars in sponsorship money. With only one stipulation."

"You," Ki guessed.

Cadge Dana laughed. "That's right. If he needs that five hundred as badly as I think he does, I'm in." Cadge was suddenly aware that he—the reporter who should have been listening—was doing all the talking. "Do you mind if I ask just who you people are? Sorry, you don't look like the scientific type to me."

Not the tall, lean man with Oriental blood. He was built like a cat, athletic and graceful. Certainly not the honey-blonde who might have been a Southern debutante: ripe body, sea-green eyes, flowing hair, perfect smile.

"Friends," was Jessica's only explanation.

"You're not going along, are you?" Dana asked.

"Yes we are."

"Another reason to convince the professor that he needs a reporter along," Dana said.

Jessica's smile deepened. The man wasn't exactly shy. He was brash and physically attractive. She recalled Sperry's doubts as to his identity. Was Cadge Dana what he said he was, a reporter?

"Do you have a letter from your editor?"

"A letter? Oh, confirming the offer of five hundred dollars. Of course," he said, casually handing Jessie a letter with the *Post*'s letterhead.

Ki asked, "You must be aware of the sabotage that's going on."

"Oh, sure." Dana took the letter back and tucked it inside his coat. "I've done a column on it. No suspects, no arrests. Nothing much as far as facts to go on. Just keeps our readers' interest up, and that's the main thing."

"No one's been caught?"

"No one. A derelict was picked up but he was just sleeping it off near the McCarthy balloon."

"You must have some idea of who's behind it," Jessica prompted.

"Some," Dana acknowledged, "but there might be a story in it. I wouldn't care to speculate right now."

Dana heard voices and, looking behind him, saw Melinda and her father, valve still in hand, walking away. "I'll be seeing you later," he said to Jessica. As a courtesy he also nodded to Ki before he took off at a half-run, calling out to Horace Sperry.

"I'd like to read what he has written about this," Ki said thoughtfully.

"Do you think he knows something?"

"Not necessarily, but he has obviously done some probing. Sperry and Melinda have only the flight itself on their minds. We know next to nothing. If anyone does know something, I'd bet it's Cadge Dana. He was a little evasive when we asked who might be behind this."

"Back to town, Ki?"

"I think so, don't you? There's no place to sleep here. I'd like a bed and a bath."

"And a look at the recent newspapers."

"Yes." Ki smiled.

To this point the project Jessica had agreed to seemed trivial. Rival balloonists trying to sabotage each other. Yet if those measures failed, what followed? If fifty thousand dollars was worth going to all this trouble, it was also worth killing for.

Something was bothering Ki, but the martial arts expert couldn't put a finger on it and name it. It was a foreboding, perhaps a concern for the lives of Professor Sperry and his lovely daughter; all Ki knew was that he was uneasy. There was a smell to this, a feeling of evil. Having no logical framework for any of his thinking, he didn't mention it to Jessica.

Yet the feeling stayed with him. *Something* was wrong here, and it went beyond petty vandalism.

Ki had learned not to brush aside such feelings. He was a warrior and a man whose physical discipline overlapped with deeper senses. Trained in a monastery, Ki was a master of *te*, empty-hand fighting. The hours he had spent following the forms of the discipline, submerging his conscious thought to the exclusion of reason as his body flowed and became, in effect, the master of his mind, had opened secret doors in his psyche. He had learned to *feel;* to sense and to trust his instincts—the instincts of a more primitive creature.

Such instincts had saved his life and Jessica's on many

8

occasions since he had been chosen by her father, Alex Starbuck, to be the millionaire's bodyguard and mentor.

Now it was there, that feeling . . .

"Ki?" Jessica said, and Ki realized he was standing beside their buggy, looking into the distance. "Did you want *me* to drive?"

"No, Jessica. Excuse me."

"Is something bothering you?" she asked as Ki stepped into the buggy and unwound the reins from the brake handle.

"Something, yes. What, I do not know."

They crossed the hills once more and entered San Francisco from the foot of Commerce Street. The harbor was a forest of masts. Sailing ships from all over the world rested at anchor there. American clipper ships from Baltimore by way of the Horn, British freighters, junks from Japan and China, Alaskan fishing ships.

Fog was beginning to drift in across the bay and the sun was reddening as it sank toward the Pacific before Jessica and Ki drew up in front of the Empire Hotel at the end of Market Street.

Ki stepped from the buggy and took their luggage from the bed as Jessie stepped out and stretched.

Ki shouldered one trunk, hoisted the other in his left hand, and started toward the door to the hotel. A man in a red uniform with coils of braid across one shoulder stepped in front of him.

Ki tried to move around him, but the doorman stopped him again. "No Chinese," the big Irishman said, pointing. "Can't you read the sign?"

There was indeed a large sign in the window of the hotel, written in English and Chinese characters. Ki bristled but only answered, "There is no problem. I'm not Chinese."

"You look Chinese," the doorman insisted.

"The sign does not say 'No one resembling Chinese,'" Ki pointed out as he tried to hold his temper.

"Smartass too, are you?" the doorman said. He had his hand in his back pocket, and Ki reasoned that he had some weapon or other there.

The doorman, whatever the cause of his antagonism, had

9

made a serious error. He saw only a Chinese with his hands filled with luggage, wearing a leather vest, headband, and cork-soled slippers. Hardly the type the Empire Hotel admitted. The woman with him was beautiful enough—astoundingly so, but she wore a flannel man's shirt and jeans, and a flat western hat. She didn't appear to be the type the hotel would welcome either. The doorman, just doing his job, had fallen into a series of errors.

None was so serious as the error he made next.

The doorman put his hand on Ki's shoulder and half turned him as the "Chinaman" was burdened with his luggage. A blackjack appeared from the uniformed man's hip pocket and he whipped it toward Ki's skull.

The doorman was never sure what he saw next. It had to have been imagination, he thought, or the Chinaman had accomplices somewhere.

The trunk dropped from Ki's shoulder, and that hand caught the doorman's wrist in a crushing grip. His thumb dug into the nerves at the base of the man's palm, and the blackjack fell to the ground as Ki's other hand drove up under the doorman's chin, a single finger driving the man backward to crash back against the wall of the hotel and sag to the sidewalk.

Before the doorman had cleared his head Ki had shouldered the trunk, hoisted the suitcase, and walked past him into the lobby of the Empire.

The desk clerk had seen a part of it, but he couldn't accept what he had seen any more than the doorman had. "What happened?" he asked excitedly, his eyes bulging from his narrow skull.

"He fainted, I believe," Ki answered. "He may have been drinking."

"My name is Jessica Starbuck," Jessie said quickly. "You have my reservation."

"*Starbuck*. Of course, Miss Starbuck!"

"And a room for my friend, Mr. Ki."

"Your friend? I assumed . . ." Nervous eyes went to the front of the hotel where the doorman was rising. "Of course. Right across the hall. Rooms two-ten and two-twelve.

The clerk was rewarded with a smile which left him staring after the honey-blonde as she walked away. It took him a full minute to realize he had forgotten to ring for the bellhop.

Once upstairs, Jessie admitted to Ki that she was sleepy, let him out, and then stripped off her clothes to stretch out on the wide, soft bed.

Ki was still determined to have a look at the newspapers, and after rinsing off he went back out into the street. He asked the doorman, "Where is the *San Francisco Post* located?"

"The newspaper? Two blocks down and right around the corner, *sir,*" the man answered quickly.

"Thank you," Ki replied, starting that way. The street was bustling with traffic; fringed surreys, heavy freight-wagons, men on horseback. On the sidewalks ladies in pairs strolled, twirling parasols. The sun was down and lights came on along the street, up on Nob Hill, down along the harbor up toward the Barbary Coast. The saloons were filled, the shops nearly empty.

Ki found the *Post,* an old brick building, and walked in. In the back of the building a press clattered away. There was a lady in a dark skirt and ruffled, high-necked blouse behind the desk, and Ki started that way to ask for their files. But the opening of a door down the corridor caused him to look that way. The door was half-windowed, and on the glass was the title EDITOR-IN-CHIEF ERNEST GALLOWAY.

"Mr. Galloway?"

Ki approached the stubby, gnarled man while receiving a curious stare. "I'm Galloway, yeah. What is it?"

"I wanted to check on the credentials of one of your people," Ki explained.

"Let me guess," Galloway said with a crooked smile. "Cadge Dana."

"That's right. How could you know?"

"It's usually Cadge. People can't believe a sane man would have hired that ex-pugilist."

"He was a fighter?" He hadn't impressed Ki that way. "Either it was a short career or a good one. The man I mean doesn't have a mark on him."

"He was good, yeah. Look, Cadge Dana is thirty-four

11

years old. Blond, good looking, always in a hurry. Yeah, he was a fighter and a merchant sailor, a bartender, and a few rumored less savory things."

"You trust him, Mr. Galloway?" Ki wanted to know.

"Trust him? Damn right. He can write and he'll go out and get a story if he has to tear a wall down. Send him down to Barbary and no one fools with him. Send him uptown and the society ladies think he's cute as a bug's ear."

"And if you send him up in a balloon?"

"Oh, that's why you're here." Galloway nodded. "That was Cadge's idea. I think he's nuts. I think they're all nuts, but it'll make good copy. You're with Sperry?"

"That's right."

"He's another one they ought to haul away to the asylum if you ask me," Galloway said. "Are you flying too?"

"Yes."

Galloway shook his head again. "I've talked to some experts on this. Anyone who thinks this is possible is crazy according to them. You've got to fly over the Sierra Nevadas or try to float through a pass in them, negotiate the desert where they tell me hot air currents will raise hell with any stability the balloon might have. Then you've only got the Rockies and another thousand miles of open country. Once the balloon is down, you're through—and likely stranded in Indian country. No chance of continuing after nightfall—that means you have to set down at night, and if you just happen to be in the mountains or in the middle of hostile country, that's too bad. Is it worth it? For fifty thousand dollars? Mister, I wouldn't tackle it for five times that."

Ki thought that was a fairly accurate summing-up of what Sperry had to go through, and of what Jessica had volunteered them for. It did sound insane, spelled out like that, but then why was Sperry so sure it was possible? He might be a little eccentric, but he wasn't a raving maniac.

"I'd like to go through your files," Ki said. "See what Dana and your other writers have to say about this."

"Help yourself. Miss Speck there will help you. I've got to get down to the composing room. Good luck to you, Mister. You'll need it."

After a brief handshake Ki was left alone to return to the desk where Miss Speck smiled meaninglessly and took him to a room filled with the past editions of the *Post*. Ki began to look through the newspapers, not really sure of what he was looking for. Something, perhaps, to explain that gnawing feeling that everything was not right here.

Jessica's eyes opened. She was lying naked on her bed, the window half open, a light sea breeze fluttering the curtains.

She wasn't alone in the room.

Chapter 2

Without seeing anyone or hearing anything consciously, Jessica Starbuck knew someone was in the room. Stretching her arms slowly she reached under her pillow. There was a little something there for any intruder.

The double-action Colt had been specially made for her, factory-ordered by her father. Slate-gray with peachwood handles, the .38 was built up on a .44 frame. It was hardly a delicate lady's weapon, but beneath her silken skin and lush body, Jessica Starbuck was far from being a delicate little thing.

She enjoyed sex frankly, could ride like a Comanche, and was leather-tough when she had to be. She had learned some open-hand fighting from Ki, enough to take care of herself if the average man tried anything funny.

And she could shoot.

The smooth, familiar grips of the .38 filled her palm, and through half-opened eyes she slowly searched the room. She saw nothing, not a shadow. Maybe she had been dreaming, bringing nightmare images into the waking world.

Then the man lunged and Jessie saw the starlight on the blade of the knife he held. The .38 came around and Jessica squeezed the trigger twice, filling the room with flame and sound. The attacker reeled back, his cry of pain high, womanish.

Jessie sat up in bed, two-handed the Colt, and prepared herself to send the finishing slug through the muzzle of the .38. She never had to fire that shot. The intruder, screaming with pain, doubled over, ran to the window, and crashed through it.

14

Jessica leaped to her feet and rushed to the window in time to see the man hoist himself to his feet and stumble off up the alley.

The knock on the door brought her head around. Ki's voice was reassuring, urgent.

"Jessica! What is it? Open the door."

Jessie slung a bedspread across her shoulders, walked to the door, which she swung open. Ki was standing there with a half a dozen other partly dressed hotel guests. Ki squeezed through the door and she closed it.

"Are you all right?" He noticed the gun in her hand immediately, the shards of glass, the smell of burnt gunpowder.

"Yes," Jessica said a little breathlessly.

"Did you see who it was?"

"No. A man."

"With a bullethole in him. Sit down on the bed, Jessica. You're still a little wobbly."

"Yes." Jessica looked at her gun and then again at the floor, where glass and blood mingled. "Funny," she said, "when you know you're going to have to fight, it's all right. But when you wake up and someone's there it's different."

"Nobody's designed to go from rest to violence. Well, they obviously know we're here," Ki said, perching on the bureau, clasping his hands.

"*Who* knows?"

Ki shrugged. "That's the question, isn't it? I don't like it, Jessica. I understand there's big money at stake here. I didn't think it was enough for them to come gunning for a sleeping woman."

"Apparently it is. Where have you been, Ki?"

"The newspaper office."

"Checking on Cadge Dana?" she asked.

"While I was there, yes. Apparently he's all right as far as his credentials go. Apparently he sniffs a bigger story than the one he's got."

"What makes you think that?" Jessica recrossed her legs and hunched in the bedspread. The night breeze had grown damper, cooler.

"Hints here and there in his columns. Exactly what he's

15

onto I couldn't say. Here," Ki said, taking a bundle of clippings from his pocket, "if you want to look through them now."

"I'm not going back to sleep," Jessica assured him. "I thought by now we'd be overrun by the police and hotel managers and guests, though."

"Not in San Francisco. They go to sleep to the music of guns."

Jessie leafed through the news clippings. A lot of them were about the scientific implications of the balloon race. There was an interview with Horace Sperry, including his moonship idea which the reporter had recorded without comment, and an interview with the race's backer, Gustav Schultz, quoted from a St. Louis paper.

"My business is beer," the brewer had said, "but my interests go beyond hops and malt. I correspond with people in New York, play chess by mail with men in Portland and Oakland. My house (described as palatial by the unknown reporter) is furnished with antiques from the Orient, from China and Japan. I do business with bankers in San Francisco.

"Now," Schultz went on, "there is little in life so frustrating as having commerce and communication delayed, having some wild Indian or outlaw in Utah take your correspondence off a stage and ignorantly throw it away—the last chess move after you've checked your opponent, say, or the latest stock market news which can cost a man like me a few dollars.

"Nor do I like to sit for months and stare at the blank wall where my Tibetan tapestry was supposed to hang for months, even years, before they arrive in tattered condition. If they do. I suppose I've furnished the Indians with some interesting booty over the years.

"The main thing is communication. When I have something to say I don't want to wait a —— year to say it, or to get a reply. Why not look to the future to solve these inconveniences? Air ships! I'd like to see a Red Indian or a *pistolero* hold up a balloon floating past a thousand feet in the air. And if I can advance science at the same stroke, well, what's fifty thousand dollars. . . ."

There was more in the same vein. Jessica skipped through a lot of it. The first article with Cadge Dana's byline was more

16

curious, more mysterious.

"The city has been invaded by a strange force out of the future: brightly colored and striped balloons designed to carry their human creators over the rugged mountains and impassable deserts at speed and altitude. Any citizen wishing to witness the start of this event on the twelfth of this month can hardly be disappointed. Brass bands and a rousing San Francisco send-off are assured.

"Just don't attempt to penetrate the security of these launching sites before the twelfth. They have guns in those hills, partners. Believe me. And there's a lot of hot air that has nothing to do with ascension. Try interviewing some of these rascals with their eye on that fifty thousand dollars."

Jessica shrugged. "There doesn't seem to be anything sinister hidden here, Ki."

"No? Read on."

"But then," the article continued, "maybe it's just *this* reporter they don't want to talk to. Our Barbary pirate Tyler P. Gregor is involved in this expedition—and someone tell me when Gregor was interested in something more scientific than fixing a roulette wheel?

"At any rate, when the China clipper *Renowned* docks in San Francisco with its shipment meant for Mr. Schultz of St. Louis, Tyler P. Gregor will take to the air to try delivering a portion of it ahead of the fleet of eccentrics and greedy aviators now busy inflating their balloons in the valley."

"He doesn't like Gregor, apparently."

"No, and this Gregor seems to have an unsavory reputation."

"Beyond that, Ki, I don't read anything here."

No, Ki thought. You don't *read* it there. But Ki *felt* something there. Cadge Dana knew something more than he was telling. He was just a little too anxious to make this flight when the entire race could have been reported—or invented —on the ground.

Morning was bright and cool. The fog had retreated to sea by the time Ki and Jessica started for the valley once more. The *Post* was on the stands with a banner headline: *Renowned* in Port."

Cresting the hills of Alameda they could see a green balloon, like the head of a rising monster pasted against the pale sky. To the south a black-and-white balloon, half-inflated, lifted itself. The great crimson airship was unmistakable. Nearly twice the size of most of its competitors, Sperry's huge handiwork dwarfed them in ambition and intent.

Sperry's crew was running in circles, tightening the pegs that held the great balloon down, throwing some equipment into the great wicker gondola, removing other gear. The tent had been struck now, and near it stood Melinda Sperry, watching with pride as the red balloon filled with hot air, and swelled.

"Hi!" Melinda called to Ki and waved. "Two hours, no more!"

"We're ready." Ki wondered if he really was as he tilted back his head and looked up at the vast form of the hot air balloon.

"The horses are on already," the woman told him.

"Horses?"

"There's enough lift, believe me. Father figured it out, and he's never wrong about that sort of thing."

"But why carry horses? Won't the weight slow us down?"

"A little on lift, but not once we're airborne. We've got the largest gondola, Ki; we must make use of it. What if we do hit bad weather or need repairs? Do you think those men like McCarthy or Chambers are going to be able to hike out and find help?"

Ki admired the logic but wondered about the practicality of the idea. Horses in a wicker gondola floating five thousand feet in the air?

"Is Cadge Dana here?" he asked.

"Cadge, oh yes," the redhead said. Her eyes and thoughts were only on the balloon, the monument to her father's imagination. "The five hundred dollars, you know. Father had decided he rather likes him."

"Where are they now?"

"Both in the gondola. With Eric, our engineer. We'll be second off the ground so there isn't a lot of time."

"Second off the ground? I assumed everyone would take off at once."

18

"In a horse race, yes. But with balloons we need a little more room, Ki." She advised him, "You and Jessica had better take whatever you need on board. The ladder's down, and if you need any help, I'll send Eric along."

Ki hadn't seen Eric yet and said so. "Has he been with you long?"

"Long? No, we hired him in San Francisco. He's very good, really. He changed the jets in the burner so we're using half the kerosene we were."

Eric might have been a good mechanic; Ki couldn't say. But he was *big*. He came forward wiping his huge red hands on a dirty rag. He was redheaded, bulky, well over six feet tall, with cold blue eyes.

"That's it," Eric announced, eyeing Ki suspiciously. "I got my gear on board. I'll go up the ladder." Before Melinda could answer, the big man ambled away. Ki saw him start up the rope ladder to the gondola. He moved easily despite his bulk.

"I'll tell Jessica what we're doing. How long do you think before we take off?"

"As soon as . . . not long now, Ki!" She gripped his arm and half turned him.

People were coming out from the city now, by the hundreds. The distant sound of a brass band drifted to Ki's ears and after a minute he saw that an entire twelve-piece band had been loaded onto two freight wagons and rattling up the road, they played, while men on horses, ladies in buggies, and scores of kids running alongside made their way toward the balloons, waving the red-white-and-blue, tooting horns, hoisting bottles. It was a grand excuse for a party.

But then everything was, in San Francisco.

Ki walked to the buggy where Jessica waited. "It'll be soon, Jessie. Melinda says we should take our things on board."

"We might be safer there," she said with a smile, looking down the hill toward the approaching mob.

Ki agreed. He unloaded their baggage and carried it to the foot of the rope ladder. Looking straight up, it seemed farther to the gondola than he had thought. The balloon, almost completely inflated, now blocked out half the sky. Ki left one trunk and started up with the other.

Again he was surprised as he stepped onto the gondola's deck. He had seen the contraption before, but now it seemed even larger. He might have been on a small ship preparing to sail, but there was no dock—and, worse, no sea to sail on but clear air.

Above the gondola's cabin roof a huffing engine sent jets of kerosene-scented flame into the bowels of the great balloon. Sperry was up there, wrench in hand, but he didn't pay any attention to Ki when he lifted a hand.

Cadge Dana, in shirt sleeves, rushed toward Ki and headed up a ladder to the engine. "Where do I put this stuff?" Ki called. Dana just pointed forward, and Ki, moving that way across the swaying deck of the gondola, found a small Chinese, impeccably attired and barbered. The man squinted at Ki, decided he was not Chinese, and nodded toward the cabin door.

Ki went in past the white-coated Chinese and put the trunk down carefully. It didn't seem a good idea to drop anything or slam doors or kick the walls. Everything was of wicker, stained dark. Hefting a cot, Ki decided it couldn't weigh more than twenty pounds.

"Everything all right?" the Chinese asked, bowing.

"Yes."

"Japanese," the man hissed, briefly showing emotion. The two countries had had centuries of war, and prejudices still ran deep. The expression faded to mild affability and the man bowed again. Ki started out for the second trunk and heard the man say another word under his breath: "Samurai."

The Chinese was perceptive enough to know a warrior when he saw one. And he had seen one.

The *te* master clambered back down the ladder as the brass band, now discharged from the wagons, blatted away and people wandered everywhere across the meadow, some of them being chased away by the ground crew for tampering with tethering lines, or even throwing rocks at the balloon overhead.

Jessica had finished hiring two men to return their rented

buggy to the stable—a simple matter. They had walked up and now, half-drunk, were grateful for the job and the ride.

Melinda ran toward Jessie and Ki, her elbows tucked into her side, hands moving from side to side, breasts bobbing. "Any minute now," she said and she pointed up the road toward the city. "That should be the mail."

And it was. Two of the three men on the wagon were obviously sailors. Their wagon carried more cargo than Jessica had expected. Rolling toward the balloon, they halted and gaped. Two sailors off the *Renowned* after two months at sea were now confronted by two of the most beautiful women on the face of the earth. It took them a long while to consider anything but feasting their eyes.

"Mebbe you got all day, gobs," the driver said, spitting. "But I ain't. Give 'em their gear. Bunch of foolishness anyway, floating to St. Louis."

"Clouds do it all the time," Melinda Sperry said.

The teamster glowered. "That's right. So do the little birdies, they tell me. This thing—" He looked deprecatingly at the balloon. "Be lucky if you all can get off the ground."

The sailors had leaped from the bed of the wagon. One bowed to Melinda and gave her an envelope with the big character "2" printed in red and handed Ki a sack the size of a duffel bag.

There was nothing in the envelope but a piece of paper with the time of launching written on it: 12:15. Melinda glanced at it, stuffed the envelope into her hip pocket, and said, "We've got something like ten minutes. Get aboard. I've got a last word for the ground crew."

Ki shouldered the sack, which was as light as he had expected, and went up the ladder to the gondola. The Chinese was there again. He crooked a finger at Ki and led him to a small storage area where the mailbag could be placed.

Ki walked around the gondola once, looking down at the ground, and waving to the people below, who seemed to expect it. The walkway was four feet wide all around the cabin, which still moved slightly. The wicker underfoot and the swaying of the deck didn't do much for his confidence. He supposed a man could get used to it. Sooner or later.

21

All along the rail, fifty-pound sacks of ballast hung. Great woven steel cable rose toward the balloon. A tangle of lighter lines spidering out from these formed a net, which retained the balloon itself.

Down a ladder from the top of the cabin slid Cadge Dana. The blonde, sleeves rolled up, face smudged, announced, "We're ready!"

Looking over the rail he waved to Melinda who spoke rapidly to her ground crew before darting toward the balloon's rope ladder. Ki returned to that side of the gondola with Dana at his heels. They helped Melinda up and in, and Ki felt the gondola lurch heavily. He braced himself and looked over the rail, noticing immediately that the people looked smaller.

It was 12:15 exactly, and the great crimson balloon was airborne.

They gained altitude quickly. Jessica, moving carefully toward Ki, joined them.

"There goes Gregor," Cadge Dana pointed out.

He was right. The black-and-white-striped balloon was slowly rising, veering toward them.

"And McCarthy," Melinda pointed out. The green balloon she indicated was still low, but rising quite quickly. The gondola was more nearly a circus-size basket used to take paying customers up for a few minutes' thrill.

"He won't be too damned comfortable," Cadge Dana said. "McCarthy and a crew of two packed into that straw pot."

Ki, shading his eyes, could see San Francisco now, and the glitter of the bay in the noon sunlight. He pointed out yet another balloon beginning its rise. It appeared very small now, its yellow silk like a bright flower against the green of the land.

"Simmons," Melinda said. "He—"

As they watched the yellow balloon suddenly tilted sideways. A line flew free and the balloon deflated. One man leaped from the basket gondola as it spun earthward. No one spoke for a minute. It was Melinda who finally did.

"Bad luck, bad luck," she said.

"Luck, hell," Cadge Dana muttered and he turned away to walk up the deck by himself.

"What did he mean? Does he suspect more sabotage?" Melinda asked.

"I wonder what he thinks," Jessica said. She looked upward, watching the mouth of the balloon. The occasional jet of orange flame rose from the burner.

Below the earth slipped past, forest and rivers, tiny farms with tinier animals and people.

"Five of us now," Melinda said. "Five balloons."

And how many of them would be left by St. Louis? If any of them were? Ki turned to look eastward, toward the distant snow-capped Sierra Nevada mountains, hoping to God that the eccentric Professor Sperry for once in his life knew what he was doing.

Chapter 3

Their speed was difficult to gauge. At times Jessica thought the balloon had come to a standstill, but looking down she saw a wagon on the road, saw it fall quickly behind them. An occasional gust of wind tilted the deck under her feet, but she was getting used to it.

There wasn't much for her to do. The professor was constantly on watch at the burner. Melinda had her charts. Dana was near the professor most of the time, and the Chinese, Sperry's cook and factotum, was always in the cabin.

Eric was around, however. The big man made many trips past Jessica as she leaned on the rail, most of them apparently unnecessary. Once she caught him standing and staring. Just staring. She didn't smile.

Jessica Starbuck was used to being stared at by men, but there were some to whom a smile was encouragement and encouragement a promise.

She was not encouraging Eric under any circumstances.

"It's a different way to see things," Ki said, coming to stand beside her.

"Almost magical."

Ki laughed. "Don't say that to the professor unless you want a lecture on science."

"Where have you been?" she asked, turning to look at Ki.

"In the cabin." He added off-handedly, "Someone has been in our gear."

"Who?"

"No idea. All I can tell you is that someone has been in our trunks."

"Did they take anything?"

"Not that I could tell. However," he said, "I've decided to keep these in my pockets."

In Ki's toughened palm was a *shuriken*, a throwing star. He tucked it away again in his leather vest and stood watching the land pass beneath them. From time to time they could see the other balloons behind them. It was impossible to tell if they were gaining or not.

Tyler Gregor's big black-and-white-striped balloon flew the highest. The others, colored dots against the sky, traveled nearly in a line.

Jessica was still gnawing on what Ki had told her. "There aren't very many of us on board. Who would go through our trunks, and why?"

"Curiosity, petty theft maybe."

"But nothing was taken."

Ki shrugged. "Call it curiosity. If someone did take anything where could he hide it? Say the Chinese or Eric or Dana—"

"Or Melinda," Jessica put in with a smile.

"Or Melinda." Ki said it as if that was nonsense, that no one so spectacularly beautiful could be involved in anything petty or larcenous. "It would be impossible to conceal the article, be it gold or a gun, whatever took his fancy."

"Or hers."

"Dana," Ki went on, "is curious by nature, a snoop by profession. Perhaps he wanted to find out who we were exactly."

"I imagine," Jessica said, looking up to where the blond man stood holding a line, "he knows exactly who we are if he's the reporter he's given credit for being."

"It doesn't matter, really," Ki replied. "Someone looked, found nothing, went away. It's going to be dark before very long," he went on, already forgetting the other business. "Where do we set down? Just anywhere?"

"No one's told me. I suspect that's just what we do—look for a field if we can find one."

Looking back at the other balloons, Ki pointed out, "And the man with the most nerve, willing to fly until it's com-

25

pletely dark, will be farthest ahead."

"Or dead trying to put down after dark."

"Or dead."

The sun was a fiery red ball low above the western horizon when Sperry, looking weary and exultant, climbed down from the cabin roof and started looking for a landing spot. The area they were passing over now was rolling hills with scattered oaks. It didn't seem there would be any problem—but then Jessica had never seen anyone try to land a balloon.

There wasn't much light left at all, only a long, fading red banner above the horizon when Sperry finally spotted the place he wanted.

"There," he said. "On that hill rise."

The burner beneath the balloon mouth had been out for some time. Now Sperry tugged at a line, which slowly opened a release valve and they could feel the gondola begin to drop as hot air was allowed to escape.

Nearer the ground their speed seemed much greater. Jessie braced herself against the rail. A gust of wind nearly lifted them over the knoll Sperry had chosen. At the last second he tugged hard on the line he held and the balloon dropped like a stone. The gondola slammed into the earth and seemed ready to roll, but it held. Eric and Cadge Dana were out of the gondola in a second, toting tethering lines, which they knotted around two oak trees.

Sperry started his burner again, explaining, "We can't let it deflate all the way. It would take all day tomorrow to expand it again. We have to leave the escape valve open a little and the burner on low."

Ki emerged from the cabin with his and Jessie's bedrolls. "The professor says we could sleep on board," Ki said. "Feel like it?"

Jessica smiled, looking upward. "I don't think so. I've had enough of flying for now."

"Worried about it taking off in the middle on the night?"

"Not so long as I'm not aboard," Jessica said, taking her bedroll from Ki. She wanted solid ground beneath her tonight.

The Chinese, whose name proved to be Wo Li, had started a fire and had coffee boiling. The sky was just about dark, but still there was no way of missing the balloons which drifted past them, going deeper into the hills.

"They'll have a time of it after dark," Melinda said.

"They mean to win," Ki observed. "Any chance they'll try flying all night?"

"Not unless they're completely crazy. Too much chance of snagging a tree or slamming into a mountain. No, none of them want the money that much."

Ki laid out his bedroll well away from the fire, although the night was going to be cool. It was a lifelong habit and had served him will in the past.

The horses, unsteady and rubber-legged, unhappy with the day's events, were led from the hatch in the gondola and left to graze. Ki walked back to the fire and had a cup of coffee. Professor Sperry was carrying on about wind currents, looking flushed and quite pleased with himself by firelight. Cadge Dana was writing something in his notebook. The Chinese was not there. Nor was Eric. Melinda, showing a better appetite than most of them, was working at a plate of stew.

Ki sat beside her. "You're not eating?" she asked.

"I haven't gotten used to this yet," Ki admitted. "It's like the first day on board a ship."

"Not to me; but then I've flown before. Where did you go, Ki?" the redhead asked, putting her plate aside. Firelight danced in her hair and caused her eyes to glow interestingly.

"I made my bed over there."

"So far from the fire? You'll be cold."

"It won't be that bad."

Melinda put her hand on Ki's knee. "Maybe not for you. Myself," she said, rising, "I always get cold at night."

Then she sauntered away, giving Ki one glance across her shoulder, and he watched her, wondering.

Cadge Dana, his shirt collar unbuttoned, wearing a coat but no hat, came over to sag on the ground beside Ki. He propped himself up on one elbow and asked, "No appetite?"

"No," Ki answered.

"Me neither. I still can't believe we were up in that thing all day," he said, nodding toward the balloon.

"It will give you something to write about."

27

"Yeah, if I live long enough to write anything," Dana said.
"Worried?"

"Damn right. I guess you couldn't have seen it today. Nobody but me did."

"I'm sorry, I don't know what you're talking about."

"The bullet." Cadge opened his palm and a misshapen bullet dropped out. "It hit the plate of the burner. Must have been fired from a hell of a ways off; all I heard was this little *ping*. I looked down and there it was."

"A disgruntled farmer. A kid."

"Or someone in one of the other balloons. Someone who's decided to get a little nasty." Dana stretched and yawned. "I believe I'll try to get some sleep. Good night, Ki."

"Good night." Ki watched as the newsman walked past the group at the fire, lifting a hand, and then he too rose. The bullet he flipped away into the darkness beyond the camp.

The stars were bright after the fire had been extinguished. The sky was clear and cold. Ki was watching the night, listening to the small sounds without really concentrating on them. That too was second nature to the *te* master, and when he heard a sound that did not belong in the night he sat up naked in his bed and narrowed his eyes, tensing.

She came out of the night like a descended angel, wearing something filmy and white, her long hair loose down her back. Melinda Sperry came beside Ki's bed and then slipped into it beside him. She kissed him once on the lips and said, "I do get cold at night."

"Anything I can do to help?" Ki asked. He put a hand on her smooth shoulder and let it run down to her waist and up the curve of her hip.

"Got any ideas?" she asked, her eyes star-bright and teasing. She sat up and slipped her gown from her shoulders. Her breasts, full and milky, bobbed into view and she smiled again, deeper still.

"Taking that off keeps you warmer?" Ki asked as she slid the gown down over her hips and tossed it aside, moving against him to cling to him.

"Sometimes," she said. "You'd be surprised."

"I see—you already feel warmer," Ki said, nuzzling her

neck just below her ear, one hand resting on her thigh, the other wrapped around her shoulders.

He was beginning to swell, to lengthen and thicken with the stimulus of her warm body. Her hand found his shaft and cradled it and she laughed out loud with delight.

"Sh!" Ki kissed her. "Someone may hear you."

"Not way off here. Now I know why you make your bed so far from camp."

Ki laughed as well then. "Not exactly." His lips trailed down across her throat to her breasts, where he teased her rosy nipples with his tongue as she lay back slackly, eyes half closed, still holding his rod, gently stroking it, running her thumb across its tip.

Ki hovered over her now and she shifted her legs, spreading them. He looked down into her eyes, kissed her mouth again, and then repositioned himself.

"You make me so wet," she said quietly.

"Do I?" Ki's finger explored the warm cleft between Melinda's smooth thighs. The lady hadn't lied. "Are you still cold?" he asked teasingly.

"Why? You have other ideas?"

"Lots of them." He kissed her breasts, left and then right, and let his lips travel down across her flat abdomen.

"I think you better put it in," she said hoarsely, "before I go mad."

"You think so?" Ki lay pressed against her, his flat chest against her breasts, nibbling her ear. She shifted just slightly and with her hand positioned his shaft.

The warmth of her cleft nudged the knob of Ki's erection. Melinda was tugging at him with her thumb and forefinger, inching him into her opening. Ki gave one deep thrust and she gasped, biting at a knuckle.

"Yes," she said, "I like it hard. Push again, Ki. Harder." She had begun to do a little pushing of her own, but Ki was happy to oblige her, shoving it in to the root as she bucked against him, her arms going around his shoulders, fingers trailing down to the cleft of his buttocks, groping behind him to touch his sack.

Ki withdrew halfway and then sank in again and Melinda

murmured, "Good, yes that's good, Ki. I knew it would be."

A small hissing sound rose from her lips and her lips parted, her teeth catching starlight. She was slack for a long minute more as Ki drove against her. Then she began to clutch at him, to roll her hips from side to side, to sway and moan.

"Do it . . . more." She continued to whisper words, half of them making no sense. Her legs lifted higher and locked at the ankles behind Ki's back as he continued, pistonlike, to thrust.

When she came it was with furious motion, biting at Ki's shoulder, her fingers digging into his flesh. Her legs were down again now and Ki, propped up between them, watched as she shuddered with pleasure, as her face softened and her eyes glowed.

It was another moment of slow, enjoyable motion before Ki came with a shudder and lay against her, stroking her breasts and thighs, her hips and shoulders, his lips administering soft kisses.

Melinda tugged the blanket up over his back and lay there holding Ki.

"Warm yet?" he asked her.

"Almost. Do you know any more remedies?"

"Of course," Ki said, touching her lips with a finger, which she kissed.

A muffled sound Ki couldn't identify drifted through the night and his eyes flickered. He lifted his head and waited.

"What is it?" Melinda asked.

"Sh!" It came again and Ki reached for his pants and his vest. "You'd better get your gown on."

"Something's wrong?" she asked, sitting up. Ki stepped into his clothes and palmed three *shuriken*.

"I'm not sure. But let's be careful."

Melinda dressed hurriedly while Ki, crouched nearby, listened intently to the sounds. "I know what it is. Stay here," he hissed.

"But I can't stay—"

"Stay here!" Ki ordered.

He was up out of his crouch and running barefoot toward the camp before the startled Melinda could respond. The sound had confused Ki at first—it wasn't one you heard every day.

An axe cutting rope.

Ki veered away from the camp proper and raced toward the great balloon which, burner still operating, hovered in the air above the grass.

The first man Ki saw didn't have an axe. He had a double-barreled shotgun in his hands, a hat pulled low over his eyes, a long coat.

"Better hold it," the man growled at Ki, but Ki didn't even slow down. The eight-bladed throwing star in his hand sang through the air and took the gunman in the throat.

Clutching at the *shuriken,* strangling on his own blood, the gunman fell back with a groan. Ki leaped over the body and ran for one of the two great oaks.

He saw the ax fall by starlight one more time and saw the balloon lurch to one side. The man with the ax heard Ki's approach and spun to fight him off, lifting the double-bitted ax overhead.

The *te* master launched himself through the air, and a leaping *tobi-geri* kick nearly lifted the man's head from his shoulders. The ax was still upraised when the intruder thudded back against the oak to slide slowly, unconscious or dead, to the ground. Ki leaped high, caught the tethering line, and found it jerked again from his hands by the balloon.

Someone was running toward him, and in a second Ki saw Cadge Dana, gun in hand, appear.

"Ki? What the hell—?"

"Give me a hand, Cadge, before we lose this thing."

Dana caught Ki by the arm and got him steadied on the ground. Tugging together they were able to raise enough force to get slack to knot the end of the mooring line to the tree. Wiping his forehead with his wrist Dana stepped back and looked around.

"*Now* will you tell me what's going on, Ki?"

"Just what you see," Ki said. "They were trying to set the balloon adrift."

"Why, for God's sake? And who are they?"

31

"You'll have to ask them," Ki said, nodding at the man crumpled up a the base of the oak.

Cadge crouched, slapped the man's face, and then shook his head. "It won't do any good to ask him anything, Ki. His neck is broken. He's dead."

"So is the other one," Eric's voice said. He came forward with a lantern hoisted high. "You play rough, friend," he told Ki.

The others, awakened by the uproar, had appeared through the trees now, Jessica tucking in her shirt, gun holstered. Sperry was in confusion, his wispy white hair sticking straight up. All he wore was his nightshirt and boots.

"What is this?" the professor asked in bewilderment. "What in the world is going on here?"

Cadge Dana told him: "A couple of men tried to set the balloon loose. Ki stopped them."

"Then where are the men? I should like to talk to them." Then his eyes fell on the dead man and he swallowed hard. "Oh . . ." He looked at Ki. "You had to . . . do that?"

"Or have my hair parted with an axe, yes. I'm sorry, but I assure you they would have killed anyone who stumbled on them. Perhaps you—or Melinda."

"Yes, of course. Do we know who they are?" The professor asked Eric, who had crouched with his lantern.

"Not me," Eric said, shaking his head.

"Henry Little," Dana said. "He's a Barbary thug. I've seen him around—usually at the police station."

"Who did he work for?" Ki asked.

"No telling. Henry would do anything for a bottle these days. I hope he drank it first . . ."

"I can't see how they found us, or how they got out here," the professor said, looking around helplessly. "They'd have to have followed us on horseback and then discovered our camp somehow."

"The answer's obvious, isn't it?" Cadge Dana said, wiping back his pale hair. "They had to have come in a balloon."

"A balloon. Yes . . ." The professor was still stunned. "It's hard to believe anyone would send men like this over to stop

32

us. Still, with the prize money being what it is . . ."

Melinda, in a heavier robe, now came up beside her father and took his arm, glancing only at Ki.

Eric grumbled, "We're not doing any good hanging around here."

"I suggest," Jessica Starbuck said, "that we not assume it's over, but that it may have just begun."

"You think they would try again?" Melinda asked.

"Undoubtedly. We're going to have to take turns standing watch from now on. That is, Ki, Cadge, Eric, and myself."

"What about Wo Li?" Melinda said. "I mean—where is he? I haven't seen him since this started."

"I seen him," Eric answered. "Sleeping still."

"Through this!"

"Sure. He just has his little smoke and then curls up to sleep. You couldn't wake him with a battering ram."

"I don't understand," Melinda said.

"Never mind. Who stands first watch?" Eric asked, looking around.

"I will," Ki replied. "Then Cadge, then Jessica."

"All right." Eric was agreeable. "I got nothing against sleep. And I mean to go get some."

He tramped off through the night grumbling to himself.

Sperry said, "I really didn't know how dangerous this was going to be. I shouldn't have let you come along, Melinda. I just didn't think. Spent too much time worrying about the balloon and not enough about you, I suppose."

Melinda patted his arm. "That's all right. I wouldn't miss this trip for anything." They turned too and walked back toward the camp.

"You two had better turn in as well," Ki advised Cadge and Jessica. "It's going to be a short night for everyone."

"Or," Jessica decided, "a very long one. Ki, you don't think they'll be back tonight, do you?"

"No. I doubt it, but we can't take the chance. Not tonight." He looked into the distance. "But they will be back. Someone has no intention of letting this balloon get through to St. Louis."

Someone.

Ki stood there silently wondering just *who*, as Cadge and Jessica—arm in arm, Ki noticed—returned to the camp. Then he settled in for a long night of watching and waiting and wondering.

Chapter 4

It took less than an hour the following morning to launch the great crimson balloon, beginning with the first dim light of pre-dawn. By the time the balloon was sailing high in the bright sky, the others in the race had been long in the air.

"Look!" Jessica pointed them out. The small dots of color ahead of them were miles out in front, floating across the golden, rolling hills toward the dark mountains ahead.

"Do you notice something, Jessica?" Ki asked.

"About the balloons. No, but . . . There's only three of them!"

"It appears we weren't the only ones attacked last night."

Melinda, standing close to Ki, peered at the balloons intently. "Gregor's still in it. You can't miss that black-and-white-striped silk. The green one's McCarthy. Blue and orange: That's Chambers." She slowly surveyed the sky. "You're right, Ki—either they had trouble launching or some-one else has been sabotaged."

"Or murdered," Ki commented quietly.

The balloon sailed on, Sperry dropping ballast now as they climbed deeper into the foothills and nearer to the high mountains. The wind in the canyons grew tricky. Sudden updrafts or cross-currents tilted and spun the balloon. Still they had difficulty gaining altitude.

"The damned gondola is just too big," Cadge Dana opined.

"No," Melinda insisted. "Not for the size of the balloon. Father's figured it time and again."

Dana shook his head once. "Maybe—but we seem to be lower every time I take a look."

"The horses may have to go," Sperry finally decided. "It's not only their weight, but it's impossible to keep them from shifting around down there, kicking at the walls."

"Want me to ask them to jump?" Dana asked with little humor.

"Tonight we'll turn them loose when we make camp," Sperry said. "I hoped to have them along for an emergency— and to show it could be done. Racing men would pay a fortune to have their horses transported from point to point, able to take part in more races."

That was a point Sperry wasn't going to be able to prove on this trip, apparently.

"Maybe you can take 'em with you to the moon," Dana said.

Melinda didn't like that remark. "You're getting awfully sarcastic, Mr. Dana."

"Sarcastic, hell—I'm getting scared."

Despite their problems they seemed to be gaining on the other balloonists. Chambers' small blue and orange balloon was being tossed one way and the other by the updrafts from the canyons below. Sperry thought he knew what their problem was.

"Unloaded too much ballast to rise and now they don't have the weight to steady the gondola."

Farther ahead, rising toward a gap in the mountains, McCarthy's green balloon and Tyler Gregor's black-and-white-striped monster seemed to be doing better, though McCarthy's rig had a little spin to it.

Ki glanced around the deck of the gondola. He had seen movement from the corner of his eye and was idly curious. In a moment he was more than that.

Moving around the corner of the cabin was Wo Li—carrying the mail sack.

Ki had just a brief glimpse, but it was all he needed. He sprinted toward the cabin, Jessica calling out a surprised question. Rounding the corner of the wicker cabin Ki caught Wo Li as he hoisted the mail sack and prepared to overboard it.

"Wo Li!"

The Chinese, his face astonished, turned toward Ki, still

holding the sack overhead. Ki leaped for the Chinese, caught his wrist and applied pressure. With his free hand Wo Li tried to throw the bag over the rail.

Ki had to let go of the Chinese and lunge after the bag, catching it with one hand as he leaned far over the rail. Wo Li grabbed Ki's legs and tried to hurl him from the gondola, but Ki bucked and the Chinese was sent sprawling back against the cabin wall.

The Chinese had a knife in his hand now, and he lurched toward Ki, holding the knife high, slashing down with it. Ki caught his wrist and flipped the man—right over the rail.

Wo Li screamed as he tumbled through the empty space below, his voice fading as he fell a thousand feet, two thousand feet—then his voice halted abruptly as he slammed into the earth. There was no question at all of the man's surviving.

The question was *why?*

"Are you all right, Ki?" Dana asked, picking up the knife Wo Li had carried, gazing at it with fascination.

"All right, yes." Ki put the mail sack down.

Melinda took his arms briefly and looked up into Ki's eyes. "What was he doing?" she asked. "What happened?"

Eric appeared, looked at the knife, and frowned. "Killed another man, did you?"

Ki stiffened but immediately regained control. To Professor Sperry he said, "This man Wo Li was trying to throw the mail sack overboard. Unfortunately he went the way he intended for the sack."

"Why would he do such a thing? I don't believe it."

"You have known him long?"

"No," the professor answered. "I hired him in San Francisco. I needed someone to help in the camp while we prepared the balloon for the race."

"I think we ought to have a look inside the mail sack," Cadge Dana said, eyeing the canvas bag, which was fastened by means of a padlock hooked through metal eyelets.

"Isn't that against the law or something?" Melinda asked.

"Isn't murder?" Eric put in belligerently.

"What's troubling you, Eric?" the professor asked.

"Nothing. Only the little Chinese was a friend of mine,"

37

the red-headed man answered. "And Ki here, he don't give a man a chance. Just kills 'em."

"Maybe," Cadge Dana suggested, "Henry Little was a friend of yours too."

"Who?" Melinda asked.

"The man with the axe last night."

Eric grumbled, "Maybe he was," and walked away.

"Open the mail sack?" Cadge asked.

"Jessica?"

"Let's risk it. I don't think we know everything that's going on here."

Cadge Dana didn't slit the bag. He fiddled with the lock with a hooked piece of wire and, grinning, opened it in a minute flat.

"A man of many talents," Ki said to the reporter.

"You pick up a few things on the police beat."

Jessica had already begun going through the sack. Now and then she looked at an address, but there was nothing obviously wrong there. They couldn't open each piece of mail and read it, but everything seemed to be in order.

"Just mail. Letters, an odd package or two," she told them, looking up.

"Then why did Wo Li want to throw it away?" Melinda asked in bewilderment.

Ki answered her. "To end the race. We can fly all the way to St. Louis and arrive first, but if we haven't got the mail with us, we've failed. That was Gustav Schultz' stipulation, wasn't it? Deliver his mail. There's no prize money for simply accomplishing the flight."

"The little bastard was a saboteur," Dana said. "Now ask who was doing the dirty work around your camp, professor."

"You must be right." Sperry ran nervous fingertips across his forehead and looked groundward as if he could see Wo Li's shattered body.

"We'd better lock this up," Jessica said, hefting the mail sack.

"But why? The man is gone now," Melinda said.

"Yes, Wo Li is gone," Jessica replied.

"But surely no one else—"

"We will all feel better if it is safely put away this time," Ki said gently. "Is there a place, Professor?"

"The large tool box, perhaps. If I empty the tools out. It has a lock and I have the only key."

"All right. Use that then."

"But it's over," Melinda said.

"Over?" Ki was grim. "I think that is has still just begun, Melinda."

They rose higher into the hills, drifting gently at times, at others being battered by cross-winds which would take their feet suddenly out from under them.

"When we get up there," Melinda said, lifting her eyes to the high mountains, "it will be a good idea if everyone wears safety lines."

Dana agreed instantly. The reporter, for all of his toughness, was getting a little green as the day went on. It was cold as they climbed, and they had to wear coats and gloves, scarfs and hats now.

There had been no sign of the other balloons for some time, but they couldn't worry about the opposition just now. Night was coming in rapidly and they had to find a place to set down—not such an easy proposition in the mountain country. Small valleys appeared and as quickly disappeared and they found themselves among craggy, bare pinnacles again.

There was little time left when Sperry, from atop the cabin, waved and pointed downward. "There, I think!" he called. "Vent line, Eric!" The professor took the line and began to let out air as Eric throttled down the burner.

They bounced twice and tilted precariously, but managed to hit their target—a small valley ringed with pines. Ki and Cadge Dana, knowing the drill now, leaped from the gondola with the heavy restraining lines and lashed the balloon down. Then they were on solid ground again, and it was a good feeling.

"Damn thing swung like a pendulum half the afternoon," Dana, slapping his gloved hands together, complained.

"Will tomorrow be any better?" Ki asked, looking toward the mountain peaks.

"I honestly didn't mind it the first day. Going over the

mountains, from what I've learned about wind currents, will be very bad."

"And very cold."

"Can it get colder, Ki? Christ. I can't wait until we're out over the desert."

Melinda came up to them and took Ki's arm. "Then you don't know as much as you need to about wind currents yet, Cadge. Believe me, the desert will be worse—assuming we can get over these peaks at all."

"Where is your father's confidence?" Ki chided gently.

"Confidence? I don't have the confidence he has at all. I simply know that he'll do this or die trying. I'm prepared for that. I'm with him all the way. Why, Ki, you didn't really think I believed in this impossible scheme, did you?"

It was sobering. Dana's face froze and Ki's mouth twitched. The samurai said, "We will make it. Why are we thinking like this now? Our second night and still we travel on. Without the saboteurs, why, it would have been a cake-walk."

When Melinda, after a grateful squeeze of Ki's arm, had gone, Dana said, "As if you believed that, Ki!"

"We have to believe it," Ki said, still looking to the mountain peaks. "We have to believe it, and so we will."

The horses were let out of the cargo compartment of the gondola. Their bridles slipped and with a pat on the rump, they were set free. There was grass and water in the valley that would be their home for the rest of their lives unless some wandering Indian found them, or they made their way back down to the foothills.

Supper was coffee and stew again. Melinda made some sourdough biscuits to go along with it and they ate without much appetite, mostly in silence.

"Sleeping away from the fire tonight, Ki?" Melinda asked, nudging him.

"Tonight I don't think so. After last night, though, I think someone should sleep on board the gondola, don't you, Professor?"

"In case of another raid? You can't believe we're going to have more bad luck. How could anyone find us here?"

"Just in case, let's say."

40

"Yes, all right. The women, perhaps."

"I'll do it," Jessica volunteered. "There's a cot in the cabin at least."

Eric said, "The lady can't do much if the balloon gets free, Doctor Sperry. Maybe I'd better stay on board too."

Jessica and Cadge Dana exchanged a glance and the reporter said, "No need to worry, Eric. I can operate the burner. I'll stay on board."

"Whatever you decide," the professor said, waving a hand. "For myself, I'm ready to turn in."

Eric and Cadge Dana were growing hostile. Their eyes could have melted butter. Melinda saw it brewing and said, "Father's first idea was a good one—I'll stay on board with Jessica. You men needn't trouble yourselves."

Cadge's expression reflected disappointment; Eric just smirked. There was trouble coming between the two, and it was obvious to everyone.

Jessica agreed with Melinda, although she seemed disappointed as well. No wonder. Dana was a good-looking man, and the honey blonde seemed taken with him.

"Melinda's right. My bedroll, Ki?"

"Yes." He gave it to her, feeling a little calmer. He really didn't want any more trouble either just now. For a little group that had spent all day in the air far from civilization, they had already had their share.

Ki wondered about Eric still. What was his background? No one seemed to know. He was a mechanic who had shown up and been offered a job. That he wanted Jessica was obvious; it was equally obvious that he wasn't going to have her.

Dana watched Eric with jealous, angry eyes. Eric was huge, strong, but Ki hadn't forgotten that Dana had been a prize fighter. If the two men tangled, it would be a battle.

For tonight, however, trouble had been averted. Ki heard Melinda whisper to Jessica, "Sorry," and then the two women made their way toward the gondola.

Eric and Dana still sat glowering at each other. Ki rose, stretched, and said, "That's enough for me for one day. Shall we all turn in?"

"Yeah," Dana growled. "Let's do that."

Eric rose, kicked at the fire once, and then stalked away.

Dana looked at Ki, who only shrugged and then laid out his own bed.

The professor, in a flannel nightshirt, asked Ki quietly, "Is something going on here? What's the trouble?"

"Professor," Ki answered gently, "has it been so long since you thought of women?"

"Oh." The professor's eyes cleared with understanding. "Oh! I hope this doesn't get out of hand. I'd blame myself."

"Don't," Ki said. "It's been going on since the first man and first woman walked the earth."

Then Ki slipped into his bed, scooting around a little to make himself more comfortable. The fire still blazed. Everyone appeared to be settled in for the night. Ki yawned and rolled over. At last a full night's sleep.

It wasn't to be.

They heard the groaning from the pine trees sometime after midnight. Ki sat up in bed, wakened from a dream of the monastery at Sendai, and rose to a half crouch.

"You hear that?" Cadge Dana whispered.

Ki nodded. The groan came again. Dana slipped from his bed, revolver in hand. It was the first time Ki had seen Dana armed.

Maybe it was the right time.

The fire still burned, and Ki rolled away from it, moving into the darkness. He was a big, silent cat in the woods, his bare feet making only a whisper of sound against the pine needles. He paused, looked back toward camp, hoping Dana wasn't trigger-happy, and listened.

The groan came again—nearer, but softer. Ki went ahead, weaving through the trees.

He nearly stumbled over the man. The stranger was lying on his back holding his head, looking up at the stars and at Ki without seeming to see anything.

Ki approached cautiously, eyes darting from point to point, fearing a trap. He crouched over the man and searched him rapidly. Satisfied that he carried no weapons he sat the stranger up and asked, "Are you all right?"

"Head."

"Who are you?"

"Art Cortez. My head . . ."

"All right. What happened? Where did you come from?"

"My head," the man who called himself Art Cortez repeated. "They tried to kill me."

Ki scooped the man up in his arms and started back toward the camp, calling out softly as he approached, "Cadge—it's Ki. Hold your fire."

"What've you got there?" Cadge asked.

"A man who calls himself Art Cortez."

"Cortez?"

"Do you know him?" Ki asked as he knelt to place the man on the ground.

"It seems to me there was a man of that name—or one like it—on McCarthy's balloon crew. What's the matter with him?"

"He says it's his head. I don't feel anything. There's no blood," Ki answered, rising.

"Unconscious?"

"He is now. He wasn't when I found him."

"I'll get some water. Want me to rouse the others?"

"There's no point in that. Just get the water. We'll see what he has to say when he wakes up."

That took almost an hour. When Cortez did come to he only made half-sense for a while. "Booted. Across the rocks. You know?" Ki sat the man up and gave him a drink of water, which Cortez choked on. Short and dark, he had bull shoulders and a scarred face.

"What happened to you?" Ki asked when the man's eyes seemed clearer, his breathing normal.

"They came and got us . . . maybe four men."

"Came and got who?" Dana interrupted. "Do you mean McCarthy?"

"That's right. I was working for him. Chief mechanic."

"Who attacked you?" Ki asked.

"I dunno. I was out getting wood. I heard somebody yell —Carl, I think. When I got back they were dead on the ground, all of 'em. The balloon was deflated, stuff thrown all over the place . . . That's all I seen. Someone cracked me over the head and somebody else kicked me while I was down. When I came around it was dark, nobody there. I started walking."

The sound of voices had awakened Sperry and Eric. They arrived in time to hear the end of Cortez' story.

"He's lyin'," Eric said flatly. "They sent him over here to sabotage the balloon."

"I ain't lying," Cortez insisted. "Think I cracked myself on the head?"

"I don't see no blood."

"Listen." Cortez looked frantically from one man to the other. "They're back there. They'll kill me if they find me. I played dead to get away, but maybe they came back. Maybe they noticed I was gone. You've got to take me with you."

Eric snorted. "Sure, take on a spy."

"I ain't a spy. I'm just scared, pal."

"We've had enough trouble already," Eric said.

"It's up to the professor," Cadge Dana decided.

"Yes," Ki agreed. "It's up to you, Professor Sperry."

"How can we just send this man away?" Sperry asked. "What do you think, Ki?"

"I don't know, I honestly don't. But I don't see how we can just turn our backs on him."

"You're both crazy," Eric said angrily. "You're asking for trouble. Take my word for it"—a finger was leveled at Cortez —"he's a spy sent over here to wreck things. Taking him on is like signing your own death warrants."

Eric, disgusted, stalked away, and the other three men could only stand and look at each other, hoping that Eric wasn't a prophet.

"All right," Sperry said at length. "You can go. God help me, I can't leave a man out in this country."

"You won't be sorry," Cortez insisted. "I promise you that."

Cadge Dana briefly flashed his belt gun. "Don't make us sorry. You won't like the result. I'll promise *you* that."

Ki returned to his bed then and lay down, but it was to be another night without sleep. He just watched, watched as the man called Cortez rolled up in a spare blanket near the fire and dozed off.

Bad, Ki thought, it was a bad situation and getting worse.

Chapter 5

The balloon ascended at first light in the deep shadows of the mountain range. The Sierra Nevadas were forbidding, snow-topped, wildly primitive.

"I think he was telling the truth," Melinda said, referring to Cortez, who leaned on the rail in silence, safety rope around his waist. "Look."

Ki did. The competing balloons were still ahead of them, but now there were only two, Chambers' blue-and-orange balloon and the black-and-white monster owned by Tyler Gregor.

"It may be," Ki said quietly. "But it could also be that Cortez was hired in the first place by one of the others. Hired to fly with them and then—assassinate them."

"And then take care of us?" she asked, swallowing hard.

"I don't know, but I assure you everyone is keeping a close eye on Mr. Cortez."

Nearing the mountains the updrafts became fiercer than anything they had encountered before. The gondola jerked and pitched, and there was nothing they could do but hang on. A blue-white peak ahead of them seemed so near that they could touch it. The mountain slope was sheer rock, streaked with snow. If they did hit it they would start tumbling down and not stop until they were in the bottom of the gorge eight thousand feet below.

Sperry was trying to jockey through a notch in the mountain, avoiding the jagged pinnacles, but the winds weren't cooperating.

"We're going to have to go all the way over," Melinda said. She shivered as she spoke. The blasting wind off the snow-covered mountains cut to the bone.

Ki looked up anxiously. It was another two thousand feet at least to the mountain crest and the balloon just wasn't rising fast enough.

Eric was moving around the perimeter of the gondola, cutting all the ballast loose. Sperry was shouting something that Cadge finally caught above the whistle of the wind, and he told the others.

"Overboard everything we can. Luggage, tools, furniture."

"How about him?" Eric growled, nodding at the dismal-looking Cortez. "He's the cause of this anyway."

"Let's get to it," Ki said, moving toward the cabin, his long safety line still in place around his waist. The cots went first, and then Ki's own trunk. If any of this helped the balloon to rise, it was imperceptible.

A sudden downward lurch brought a curse from Dana. Jessica fell to the gondola deck.

"Son of a bitch!" Eric yelled. "No!"

"What happened?"

"The burner's out. Damned butterfly valve!" The mechanic was scrambling up the cabin when a gust of wind took his feet out from under him and he went overboard, banging into the rail as he fell.

"Get him! Not you, Cadge!" Ki shouted. "Get that burner started."

Ki had hold of Eric's lifeline. The engineer was fifty feet below them, nearly lost in mist. He couldn't have been more than ten or twelve feet above a jutting ledge of rock, and he was obviously unconscious. Ki braced himself and started two-handing the man up. Jessica was behind him after staggering halfway down the deck, and now she too took a hand, drawing Eric up with painful slowness.

The wind tilted the balloon again and they nearly lost it. Another degree or two and they would have joined Eric, suspended from their own safety lines.

Ki was perspiring despite the cold. His hands were raw, the muscles in his shoulders popping with the exertion. Finally, leaning out, he was able to get a hand on the seat of Eric's trousers and tug him up and over the rail.

The red-headed engineer lay unconscious on the deck of the gondola. As Ki bent over to see to him he was again knocked to his feet. There was a popping sound from above them, and a flash of flame. The burner had been started again and now the balloon was slowly rising.

"Look!" Jessica called out, pointing at the vast, jagged peak before them. "My God, Ki, we'll never get over it."

"Keep throwing things overboard. Everything."

Melinda was already doing that, staggering across the deck with her arms loaded with everything that was loose. Cortez, his eyes wide, was doing even more than that. He was literally ripping the gondola apart, doors, fittings, toolkits all went overboard to lie strewn on the slope below.

He grabbed for the toolbox containing the mail sack and they had to stop him. "Not that," Melinda screamed. "Everything but that."

"Our lives are at stake here, dammit!"

Melinda repeated, "Everything but that, you hear me?"

Cortez started ripping a metal ladder from the side of the cabin instead. Even that wouldn't be enough, Jessie knew. She could hear the pop and hiss of the burner, wide open now, filling the balloon with hot air, but it wasn't going to be able to get them over the range either.

The gondola twisted around and thudded into the side of the mountain, knocking everyone down. It scraped along the side of the slope, ripping material from the gondola. Most of the rail was missing on one side now.

They came away from the mountain and then hit it again, harder yet, and the gondola groaned.

Ki held onto Eric and just watched. What else was there to do? They swung toward the mountain a third time, but this time they had a little luck. A deep canyon, unseen before, opened up and the gondola raced into it, rising slowly, steadily. There was a chance.

They clung to the rail, all of them, watching the approaching ridge.

"Brace yourselves," Ki said. "We're going to hit that too."

In a minute he was proven right. The gondola struck rock again and scraped along the ground, bouncing and creaking,

47

rattling, and pitching from side to side. Snow flew up from beneath the gondola as it was dragged across the plateau beyond the ridge by a fierce mountain wind.

And then, impossibly, they were above it, over the mountain, through the canyon, descending toward the desert beyond in their battered gondola.

"Never again, no more," Cortez was saying. "Wherever we put down next, I'm leaving. Walking out. I don't care what happens to me."

"I knew you were a coward," Eric grumbled. He was sitting on the deck, rubbing his head.

"Coward! I just happen to have a few brains. What the hell do you know anyway? You were out cold the whole time."

"Yes, well, now I'm not," Eric said belligerently. He rose to his feet as if to fight, but he sagged to the deck again, muttering, "When I'm on my feet again . . ."

"We don't really need this, Eric," Melinda said in a voice which was both soothing and authoritative. "There must be someone you can get along with."

"It's not my job to get along with anyone. It's my job to keep that damn burner working."

"Didn't do much of a job if it, did you?" Cadge Dana taunted.

Eric just stared at him. Then, finally rising, he moved heavily along the deck to clamber up to where Sperry, obviously shaken, tended the burner.

The desert was pale brown, seen through a bluish haze. Far below it rose toward them rapidly as Sperry began his descent. The air grew warmer and Ki was even able to take his coat off and toss it aside. He looked back once toward the mountains and shook his head.

"Well, that's over," Jessica said with relief.

"Until we come to the next range," Ki said.

"The Rockies are up there—if we make it that far," Dana put in, looking into the far distances.

Melinda scolded them lightly, "You all sound like you're ready to walk out of here."

"No," Ki answered, "we aren't ready to do that—but you have to admit that Cortez has a point."

"*He* made it," Dana said, pointing into the distances. And

he had indeed. Tyler Gregor's great black-and-white-striped balloon, now far below them and to the south, scudded across the desert effortlessly, like a striped cloud.

"Anyone see Chambers?"

"No."

Melinda said quietly, "I hope to God he made it."

Dana was surprised at the emotion and said so. "Cheering for the competition now?"

"No. I just wouldn't want to think of anyone going down on that mountain slope, would you?"

They raced across the desert at an altitude of a thousand feet. The land was barren, trackless. Outside of the mountains, now shrinking behind them, they could see nothing but flat, empty land. There were no structures, no animal life, no human beings.

"Still want to walk out of here?" Dana asked Cortez.

"Sure," Art Cortez said nervously, but it was obvious that his old fear was fading, being replaced by a new fear, the fear of trekking out of the desert under a hot sun. The desert already had countless victims to its credit. Along the old trails, broken wagons and ox skulls abounded. The sand drifts could be thirty to forty feet high, and there was water nowhere.

And there were the Indians.

There were the Monos, relatively peaceful, a small tribe; and the Paiutes—not so peaceful at all. Ki had even heard of Apaches this far north.

All in all it was enough to make a man reconsider walking away from the balloon.

They sailed on, picking up speed as the desert wind built. They couldn't gain distance on the big black-and-white balloon, nor could they open up a gap between themselves and Chambers' blue-and-orange balloon, which had appeared from the north to Melinda's apparent relief.

"Maybe we don't want to be too close to either of them," Cadge Dana said. At Melinda's curious glance he added, "You haven't forgotten that one of them is manned by cutthroats. Seems to me that tonight we ought to make sure we're camped well away from both of them, even if it means letting them get ahead."

"I'll talk to Father," Melinda answered. "But I know he'll

want to go on as long as possible."

The desert was all sand now, rippling dunes which appeared much smaller than they were. If they were going to set down early, Jessica thought, this would be a good area to do it in. A soft landing and visibility for miles.

"How do we moor the contraption out here?" Ki wondered.

"We just have to deflate more," Melinda said. "We did have a grappling hook and heavy anchor—but they're back there on the mountainside somewhere."

In the end Sperry compromised. He traveled on until nearly sunset, but set down much earlier than the light forced him to. The landing was soft, although the gondola was dragged for a good fifty feet through the sand.

As Sperry deflated the balloon further than it had been since the San Francisco takeoff, the others got out, examined the battered gondola, and looked skyward to see Chambers' blue-and-orange balloon sail past.

"That'll put Father in a bad frame of mind," Melinda said.

"It's much better," Ki replied. "We don't have much chance of winning the race if we're dead."

The thought chilled Melinda a bit. Art Cortez stood on the crest of a sand dune, blue and deep purple in the sunset light, looking in all directions.

"I'll lend him a telescope if he wants," Eric growled. "Where's he think he's going, anyway?"

"He just wants to get away from trouble—who doesn't?" Cadge Dana asked.

"Just like you, ain't he? Both yellow."

"Yellow, by God—!" Dana might have gone after his throat then, but Jessica's hand on his arm calmed him.

"Yeah," Eric persisted. "And maybe you're a spy like he is. I still don't swallow that tale of his."

Art Cortez was near enough now to hear that and he said, almost pleadingly, "I'm not a spy or a saboteur. Believe me!"

"Sure," Eric said cynically. "I got work to do," he said, and turned to clamber back up on the gondola.

"What the hell's the matter with him anyway?" Dana asked.

"I'll tell you what I think," Jessica Starbuck answered. "I

think he's as scared as the rest of us and that's the only way he knows how to express it."

"Let him express it on somebody else," Dana snapped. "I won't take much more of it, I really won't."

Dana too stormed away, walking out alone into the desert to cool off a little.

"Ki?" Jessica turned to the *te* master. She didn't have to say any more. They had been together a long while, these two, through many battles, and he knew what she meant. They were in a dangerous place—that huge scarlet balloon was visible for many miles. If there were anyone around they couldn't miss seeing it. The Indians would have found the sight remarkable. If Chambers and Gregor hadn't gone on as far as they believed, they might have company—dangerous company.

"I'm going to go out and look around a little while there's still light. I think everyone ought to be armed—if we can keep them from shooting each other."

"It's getting a little nasty, isn't it?" Jessica said, looking at Eric on top of the gondola with Sperry and then at Dana, hands in pockets, shuffling off across the dunes, and at Art Cortez, who was nervous, bewildered.

"Something's going to erupt sooner or later. Let's just try to keep a lid on it for now," Ki replied.

"If it weren't for Eric—"

"If it weren't for Eric, I doubt we would have made it this far," Ki pointed out. "Mechanically he knows what he's doing. If anyone has had the chance to sabotage this journey, it's been our mechanic, and he hasn't done it."

Jessica was less trusting. "Of course, Ki, he couldn't do much, could he? Not unless he wanted to go down *with* us."

"Maybe you're right. I certainly don't like the man. We'll have to wait and see—and keep an eye on him."

"And on Cortez."

"Yes."

"And Cadge?"

Ki replied, "You seem to be doing that job well enough, Jessica Starbuck."

She laughed in response. "Darn it, Ki, I like the man. You

51

know I do. Still, I feel as you do. He's holding something back. There's still something he knows or suspects about all of this that he hasn't told us."

"And that in itself could be as dangerous as saboteurs and assassins. We need to know all there is to know, Jessica. Maybe you can work on him."

The beginnings of a smile caused the corners of Jessie's mouth to turn upward as she watched the big blond newsman. "Maybe I can," she agreed.

Ki, uncharacteristically carrying a Winchester repeater, left the camp, climbing up a mountainous dune. He trudged, moving in a wide circle through the sand, his shadow long and crooked against the sunset-hued sand. He saw nothing more than Art Cortez had seen.

He found an arroyo thick with dead willow and followed it for a way as day faded. There were chocolate-colored rocks along the streambed, reminders of a flash flood that had once swept down the arroyo. Catclaw and mesquite grew in scattered areas, and Ki saw a single black-tailed jackrabbit that might have never seen a human being. It didn't feel threatened enough by Ki to lope away until Ki was within fifteen feet of it.

There were no tracks of man or beast in the river bottom. There was no sight of the other balloons, which should have been visible if they were nearby.

Somewhat satisfied, Ki made his way back toward camp through near darkness, and sat down on the sand to eat the food Melinda had prepared.

Stew and sourdough bread.

"When we get to St. Louis," Ki commented, "I intend to have everything, anything a restaurant has on its menu but stew."

"*If* we get there," Cortez said.

"We will get there," Professor Sperry promised. "If it weren't for these other . . . animals, I would have no doubt whatsoever. Gentlemen, ladies, we have passed into a new age. We are making history, proving that what no one believed possible is indeed inevitable."

At that moment no one cared to share the professor's visionary ecstasy. They were fatigued, battered, and now growing cold as the desert night came on.

"It's time to turn in," Eric said. "I'm staying in the gondola tonight—unless there's an objection."

"None at all," Ki said. Eric was a bomb waiting to go off and Ki tried to make his voice soothing. No matter what kind of bastard he was, it was obvious after a few days that they needed the mechanic.

"I'll sleep out," Cadge Dana said. "The sand's got to be more comfortable than the cabin, with the cots gone."

The others gathered their blankets and stretched out in various places. Ki had decided to stand watch for four hours although he was exhausted. The events of the last few nights hadn't done much to convince him it was safe for them all to sleep at once.

He walked up the high dune through the ankle-deep sand and perched, Winchester across his knees, ready for a long night's watch.

Cadge Dana went to the north of the gondola and found a little hollow where he spread out his blankets. He was in a sour mood; things were going even worse than he had expected.

Suddenly they got better. A hell of a lot better.

Jessica Starbuck came to him. The moon was behind her and she seemed a pale-haired dream walking toward him, her head high, hair loose, blouse loose over her perfect, full breasts. She sat down on his blankets beside him.

Cadge had removed his shirt, and Jessica rested a hand on one of his muscular shoulders as she sat beside him. His chest, square and thick, showed a few scars by moonlight. It was a man's chest, and Jessie could sense the power about him.

"What brings you out here?" Dana asked.

"A little talk." Jessie smiled. The desert wind drifted her long hair and it touched Cadge's bare shoulders and back lightly.

"Yes? What do you want to talk about?" He bent his head and kissed her neck lightly.

"I'm beginning to forget," she admitted.

"Good. Forget all about it." His hand went to her breast, manipulating her taut nipple through the light fabric of her blouse as Jessica rested her head against his shoulder.

Her breasts were full and firm, and the contact caused a stirring in Cadge's loins. He looked into her eyes and kissed her parted, supple lips.

"I can't forget it entirely, Cadge," Jessica said as her hand came to rest on his thigh. "You're keeping something to yourself."

"I'll gladly share," Cadge joked.

Jessica glanced at his crotch and laughed. "I meant something you know about this race, something you haven't told Ki or me. It can be dangerous for all of us if we don't know the whole story."

"I don't know the whole story," Cadge said evasively as his hand popped open the first button on Jessica's jeans and slid inside his fingertips, finding her downy bush, slowly stroking her vulva.

"There is something..." Jessica lay back on the sand. "Damn, I'm a lousy investigator!"

Cadge's fingers found her cleft and the erect tab of flesh there, and he gently manipulated it.

"Darn jeans," Jessica said, and in seconds she had shimmied out of them to lay back on his blanket, watching the stars, the soft glow of the moon, the face of the man over her. She closed her eyes then for a moment, enjoying his gentle probing, his finger dipping inside of her damp slit.

She unbuttoned her blouse and sighed as Cadge kissed her breasts, taking one nipple between his teeth, biting it lightly. The questioning apparently was over.

Cadge Dana stood up and removed his trousers. His erection sprang free and Jessie's hands ran up his thighs, fingers reaching for it. He knelt beside her and she kissed his manhood slowly, her tongue working against his flesh, until abruptly she rolled onto her hands and knees, and her glorious, sleek buttocks were thrust toward Cadge Dana, who knew what to do with an opportunity.

He eased in behind her as Jessie, her head twisted to one side, her hair spread out against his blanket, reached back between her legs, touching him, spreading herself, taking him in deeply.

Cadge found himself trembling as his pelvis thrust forward. He held himself still, his hands on her buttocks. Then, inevitably, he began to stroke against her, to move from side to side and drive into her, his hands moving up her spine and back as she shuddered and made small contented sounds deep in her throat.

Jessie's hand found Cadge where he entered her, and her fingers added still more stimulation to Cadge Dana's swollen need. He arched his back, hooked his hands around her thighs, and held her against him, his strength overpowering, his manhood deep and satisfying to Jessie, who smiled in the moonlight and looked back to watch as his shaft slid in and out of her, lifting her to a shuddering climax.

Dana followed her in seconds, excited by her soft moans, the wetness of her body, the heat of his loins.

He came quickly, roughly, driving her against the blanket as he filled her with his own pleasure and then collapsed against her, stroking her body as the pale desert moon rose higher.

Jessica, content, liking the weight of the man against her, closed her eyes and cat-napped for a moment, planning on waking up, trying all over again, reaching new heights with the ex-boxer . . . after she had questioned him again . . . after . . . She yawned.

The gunshots roused her and cancelled all thoughts of another bout of lovemaking. She grabbed for her Colt and her clothes in that order. A cry of pain rose on the desert wind and the stab of flame from a nearby muzzle flash blinded Jessica Starbuck as she two-handed her pistol and fired back at the unseen enemy.

And Cadge Dana pitched forward on his face, blood streaming from his side.

55

Chapter 6

His warrior's instincts outracing his logical mind, Ki assessed the problem in split seconds. His instincts told him several things rapidly.

They had been attacked, they were outnumbered, the enemy was very good.

Ki had been sitting watch on the dune and he had seen no one coming, heard nothing. That meant they were excellent indeed, these attackers. Ki's senses were keen, trained through years of martial arts work, honed through a life of danger. Yet these men, whoever they were, had eluded his perception.

Indians.

It had to be Indians. No white man without extensive training moved so softly, so secretly. To find an army of such men was nearly impossible.

The gunshot rang out before Ki could react. He started toward the gondola, tossing his own rifle aside. He wasn't going to shoot at targets that would be indistinct even with the moonlight. He would not risk killing one of his own people.

When the Paiute reared up in front of him like a devil out of the sand, Ki slashed across the man's throat with the edge of his hand and the Indian toppled backwards, rolling down the sand dune, his trachea crushed.

Someone burst out of the gondola and ducked back in immediately as a hail of arrows searched for flesh. Paiutes swarmed over the gondola, perhaps ten of them, and Ki, his heart in his throat, raced toward it.

Melinda was there, and Jessica. He had reminded everyone

to be armed on this night, but Melinda was hardly a marksman. Probably she was incapable of killing a human being.

Jessica was more equipped to handle confrontation, but one woman alone wasn't going to hold back a horde of Indians. Ki found his way blocked by a second Paiute. The man hesitated a second too long—perhaps Ki, barefoot, shirtless, his dark hair sawn off at the shoulders, looked a little too much like an Indian for the warrior to be sure.

He would never be sure of anything again. A humming *shuriken* sliced through the air and embedded itself in the Paiute's eye. Shrieking, slapping at his bloody eye, the Indian fell to the ground, already close to death.

Suddenly the attackers were gone. Leaping from the gondola, they vanished into the desert. Eric, sixgun in hand, was on the deck, aiming a few last futile shots after the vanishing Indians. There wasn't a chance in the world of hitting one of them.

"Melinda!" Ki called out.

The redhead waved a hand from the rail. "I'm all right, Ki."

That was all he wanted to know. Racing toward Cadge Dana's sleeping place across another dune, he came upon Jessie trying to stanch the flow of blood from a gunshot wound through Dana's side. In much pain, Dana writhed and doubled up.

"How bad?" Ki asked.

"I can't see a darn thing! Help me carry him, Ki."

"They gone?" Dana managed to ask.

"For now."

"They won't . . . come back?" he asked, his voice broken by a deep cough.

"I don't know. Come on now, don't worry about that." Ki put one of Dana's arms over his shoulder while Jessica supported his other side. Dana, his head lolling on his neck, was half dragged back toward the gondola.

Melinda met them before they reached it and said, "I'll make a bed inside. I'll find a lantern."

She turned and ran ahead of them across the sand toward the gondola as Ki and Jessica hurried on with their burden.

57

Professor Sperry, bewildered, wearing nightshirt and boots, caught up with them.

"What's happened?" he asked endlessly. "What's happened?"

"Get a rifle and stand watch," Ki ordered. "Indians."

"Indians! But—"

"Get a rifle!"

"We've got to take to the air, not matter if it's dark or not," the professor said. "The land ahead of us is empty. We can do it by this moon."

They were carrying Dana up onto the deck of the gondola. Eric was above them, pistol still in hand. "Got the son of a bitch, did they?" he said smugly.

"Shut up, Eric," Ki said angrily. It wasn't the time for petty disputes.

Cortez, holding a rifle, was at the rail, literally shaking. "Are they gone? Are they gone?" was all he wanted to know.

"For now."

Ki and Jessica took Dana into the cabin, where Melinda had lit a kerosene lantern, and hastily improvised a bed. They could hear the professor shouting out on the deck, "Eric, we're going to take off! Do you hear me?"

Ki left Dana in the care of the two women amd went back on deck. "Damn it all," he muttered as he noticed what no one else apparently had. He made his way toward the cabin roof where the professor, still in his nightshirt, had already fired up the burner.

"We can't go," Ki said, putting his hand on Sperry's wrist.

"But why not? We have to!"

"The mail sack," Ki said. "The Indians took it."

"But they can't have! Why? Why would they take it?" Sperry asked, his voice nearly a wail.

"It was the first thing they came across. Maybe they thought it was valuable. At any rate, they've got it, and if we take off it's all over."

"What can we do, then?"

"Get it back," Ki said quietly, taking a deep, slow breath as he looked out the the endless desert. "Just go get it back."

"Ki! Sperry was astounded, his voice nearly breathless.

"You have to be joking. It's crazy."

"It isn't something I want to do," Ki said. He took a deep breath and looked out toward the desert. "But if we don't get it back, what's the point in going on?"

"I won't let you kill yourself for my sake," Sperry said.

"I don't intend to be killed, Professor Sperry."

"I admire your courage, but—"

Ki interrupted, "You had better be ready to take off when I get back. Night flying is preferable to staying in this camp tonight, is it not?"

"Yes . . ." The professor, still stunned, waved a hand weakly. "All right, then. We'll prepare the balloon. I still think you're mad, Ki, but—good luck to you. Be careful, please."

Ki started off without another word. He didn't want to talk to Melinda or even Jessica about this. Both of them would have tried to convince him not to do it.

Oddly, despite his knowing he was moving into danger, Ki didn't feel deep concern. Probably the raiders were a small band. Hunters, perhaps, who had seen the balloon and come to investigate. Certainly there hadn't been an overpowering number of them attacking the camp. A force of a dozen could easily have overwhelmed the balloon's crew.

Now they would look for a spot to stop and search their booty. They wouldn't go far. They would expect no pursuit— or so Ki's thinking went. Maybe it was wishful thinking.

The tracks the Indians had made were clearly visible by moonlight, and they gave some support to Ki's theories. There were only five sets of footprints. Would they travel back to a larger camp before opening the mail sack? Ki thought not. Most men are greedy. They would share whatever they found among themselves while they were few.

Ki broke into a dogtrot, moving effortlessly across the sand, which was not deep on the flats where the Indians had gone. The moon floated along beside him as he dipped into the brushy arroyo he had seen earlier and ran on across a stretch of rocky ground.

A sound brought Ki to a halt, and a moving shadow took him to his belly. He had found the camp.

59

He crawled to the crest of a low knoll and looked down into the hollow on the far side. Five Indians crouched around a tiny fire. Mail was strewn about the ground, some of it opened. A few small parcels, open now, held their attention. Ki couldn't see what they were examining as they joked about, but so long as it held their attention it didn't matter.

His hand dipped into one of the inner pockets of his worn leather vest and emerged filled with the cool deadly steel of *shurikens*. Ki noted each man's position relative to his weapons, gauged the distance, and rose from the sand like an avenging demon.

The first two Paiutes never knew what hit them; they saw nothing, heard no one. The first Indian took a star-dagger at the base of his skull and pitched forward into the fire. Before any of the other raiders could react, a second throwing-star ripped through the throat of another Paiute.

The other three dove for their rifles. Ki, upright now, his targets silhouetted against the firelight, unleashed a third *shuriken* and saw a man, rifle raised, sag back to the ground.

Muzzle flashes from the guns of the remaining Indians sent Ki to his belly. He rolled to one side and then, instead of retreating, he charged at the Indians, who had expected nothing like that.

Ki launched himself into the air, his foot smashing into the throat of a Paiute as a gun went off nearly in his face. The bullet whipped past his ear.

The Indian to Ki's right tried to break his skull with the stock of his Winchester. Ki ducked and, coiling, struck out with a middle-knuckle punch, a *nakadate*, which caught the Paiute at the V where his ribs met, driving the air from his body, stunning his heart. Still the Indian had enough strength to reach for his belt knife.

Ki blocked the upward thrust of the knife with a *gedan-barai* movement and kicked out savagely. His side-kick smashed the Indian's nose.

The Paiute dropped like a stunned ox and lay still on the sand.

Ki was suddenly the only moving thing on all of the wide desert. He dragged one Indian from the fire and began collecting the stolen mail.

The object the Indians had been laughing over was at his feet. It was a small jade Oriental figure with a huge erect phallus. So Schultz, the beer baron, had other interests in life besides his brewery.

Ki collected the mail, his eyes always on the still-living Indians. He shouldered the sack and got out of there, jogging back toward his own camp, which he easily spotted. The balloon, like a dark Goliath's head, peered at him over the dunes.

He had no sense of security, not yet. He could be wrong in his assumptions still. There could be fifty or a hundred Indians out there, enraged, ready to strike back at this intruder.

Eric met him with a loaded, cocked rifle. "It's me," Ki said.

"Got it?"

"Yes."

"How many did you have to kill this time?"

Ki ignored the man. He clambered up into the gondola and placed the sack back in the toolbox where it had been stowed.

Melinda was there suddenly, in his arms, and she kissed him, stroking his hair. "That was foolish, really foolish, Ki."

"It's done now. How's Dana?"

"He'll be all right."

"When can we take off?" He glanced back at Eric, who was climbing over the rail.

"Any time. Is there a rush now?"

"We don't want to be here if we don't have to be," Ki replied. "Tell your father we're ready."

They lifted off the ground five minutes later and at low altitude sailed across the desert. It was a wonderland by moonlight, the wind-sculpted dunes like frozen breakers, tinted blue, with gold at their crests.

Jessica was with Dana, who slept fitfully. The bullet, she told Ki, had grazed his ribs painfully. "He's lost blood, but he's strong. I don't think there's a real problem. Yet you never know with gunshot wounds, and I wish there was some way to see a doctor."

"We might manage that yet," Ki answered. "Melinda thinks we just may try to set down near a town in the morning. There's a place called Wallace that is right on our line of travel."

"I've never heard of the town. It would be amazing if they had a doctor."

"I know, but there will be some sort of medical supplies, maybe a barber. Our food supply is low; the gondola is falling apart. We need to make a few repairs if we're going to continue."

"What about the competition?" Jessica asked, resting a hand on the sleeping Cadge Dana's bandaged chest.

"We have to assume they've had some problems too. If they haven't, well, they're on their way to victory. If they decided to fly tonight too, they are well ahead."

"Poor Sperry."

"You can't dampen his enthusiasm. I think he's really in this for the sake of science. He needs the money to go forward with his projects, but I also think he would have done it for nothing."

Bleary-eyed at sunrise, they saw the sun, vast and red, back-lighting a squalid, scattered town of adobes and weather-grayed huts.

"I wonder why anyone would want to live out here," Melinda said. "In the middle of the desert."

"They probably wonder why anyone would want to go flying across the mountains in a hot-air balloon," Ki answered.

"If anyone's up this early, you can bet seeing us come in will be the biggest surprise of their lives."

"I don't think so," Ki answered. He lifted a finger and pointed to the south of the town. Chambers' blue-and-orange silk was spread out across the ground, draped over the gondola of his balloon.

"I'll be damned," Eric muttered. "We ought to go over and crack their skulls for them."

Melinda was shocked. "Eric!"

"They tried to kill us, didn't they—back there. They might have killed Cortez' people, if you can believe his story."

"And," Ki pointed out, "they may have had nothing to do with it at all—there's always Tyler Gregor."

"Should we set down?" Melinda asked.

"No choice now. Besides," Eric said, "I don't have it in me to go all day after last night and I don't think your father does either."

"We have to get some help for Dana too."

"Ki." Melinda took his arm. "Don't let there be any trouble with Chambers' crew."

"Believe me, more trouble is the last thing I want," Ki told her.

"Eric?"

"They come looking for it, they'll find it."

"Don't you go looking for it, all right?" the redhead pleaded.

Eric just repeated his remark. "If they come looking . . ." Then he went to help the professor bring the balloon in.

"Chambers must have had serious trouble for him to deflate completely," Melinda commented. "Maybe they ran out of fuel for the burner."

"Yes." Ki was still looking at Eric. "Maybe Eric ought to stay out of town completely. We can leave him to guard the balloon."

"He won't like it."

"He's working for you, isn't he?"

Melinda shrugged. "I wonder."

They came in low. The gondola barely skimmed the tips of a row of mesquite bushes along a dry river-course and landed in a pasture behind the town. A group of small boys and girls, most of them barefoot, were clustered around the balloon before they had settled to earth. They shouted questions, pointing.

Ki went to help with Dana, but he was on his feet—shaky, pale, but on his feet. Jessica helped him slip into a shirt. She asked Dana, "What does this Chambers look like? I could walk right into him and not know who he was."

"He'd be hard to miss. Walt Chambers used to be a sailing captain—some say a privateer. He's just about bald but wears a huge yellow mustache. His nose is pushed over to one side."

"What's he do now to make a living?" Ki asked.

"Cattle . . . some say he's a privateer in that business as well," Dana said, wincing as he tried to tuck his shirt in.

"A rustler, you mean?"

"I don't know. I'm just telling you what goes around."

Melinda appeared in the cabin door. "Are we ready?" she asked.

63

"I think so."

"Eric's going to stay behind," the redhead told Ki. "He and Art Cortez."

"Cortez? I thought he'd jump ship here, settle down in this nice little community."

"He hasn't said another word about it. Ki—you don't suppose someone did send him over, that he is a saboteur or spy?"

"That the other, his talk about leaving, was just a little camouflage? It could be, I suppose."

The professor, knotting a red tie around his neck, appeared in the doorway. "I hope they have kerosene in this godforsaken place," he said.

"How about the gondola?"

"I think we'll have to do most of the repairs ourselves. I don't have any hope of finding someone who could do that work. After looking it over I think we can wire it up well enough."

They went over the rail, Dana moving gingerly. After waving to the children, they started toward the drab little town of Wallace.

In front of a hardware store, which was still closed, they found a man tilted back in a chair, smoking his pipe in the morning sunlight.

Ki asked him, "Have you got a doctor in this town?"

The man looked him over, turned his head and spat. "Nope." He continued to stare at Ki, "What are you—Indian, Chinese or what?"

"Half Japanese, half American."

The man spat again. Jessica tried a smile on him. "My friend's been hurt. Is there anyone in town who practices medicine?"

It took three puffs on the pipe before the local found the will to answer.

"Henry. The barber. He's all right if you don't let him leech you. I let him leech a black eye I had once. Really puffed out—"

"Does this store carry kerosene?" the professor interrupted.

"Not this one. General store, over there. Ain't open, though. Not until eight."

"Thank you," Jessica said, and they started up the street.

64

The man stared after them all the way down the block. *That* was an odd bunch. Two young ladies in pants, an old man, a young man, and an Indian. He shook his head at the marvel of it, spat, and leaned back to puff on his pipe.

"We're going to have to wait awhile, it seems," Jessica said. "Any ideas on how to kill time?"

"Any ideas!" Cadge Dana said. "Can't you smell that, Jessie—someone in this town is frying ham."

"Breakfast?"

"That's right. Ham, eggs, coffee, hotcakes—anything but stew and sourdough."

"I thought you were sick," Melinda said.

"That bullet didn't hit my stomach, lady."

The restaurant wasn't hard to find. When they entered they found half a dozen men, two of them in business suits, sitting at the long plank table while a harried waitress rushed in and out of a steaming kitchen. Their party drew a few glances and under-the-breath comments as they made their way to a back table and sat down.

Breakfast was hot and plentiful, the coffee dark and bitter. Dana proved that he did indeed have an appetite, demolishing his food.

Ki was fishing in his trousers for a couple of silver dollars when the front door opened and a trio of men came in. He knew who they were, knew it before Dana muttered, "Walt Chambers."

"That's all right. Ignore them," Melinda said.

That was exactly what Ki meant to do—if Chambers let them.

But the man with the huge yellow mustache wasn't going to do that. He said something to one of his men and tramped across the room to stand directly in front of their table, glaring down.

"You Sperry?" he asked.

"I am," the professor answered calmly.

"We got some things to talk about."

"Do we? What, for instance?"

"*What,* for instance, why you damned old fool—killings and sabotage, for instance!"

Chambers' voice rose to a roar. His face was growing red-

65

der by the second. Melinda tried to calm him down.

"Why don't you sit with us and have some coffee—"

"I'm damned if I will. I know what's been happening, and by God, somebody is going to pay for it."

It was then that he whipped out his revolver, scattering the restaurant's patrons.

Jessica was nearest to Chambers, and she acted. The side of her hand came down hard against Walt Chambers' wrist and they heard bone snap. The gun fell to the table, and Chambers reached for it with his other hand. Jessica kicked him just below the knee and then came to her feet, driving her knee into his groin. Chambers fell back, howling, clutching himself.

"This ain't over!" he bellowed as his men came forward with drawn guns.

"Yes it is," someone said quietly. One of the business-suited men had remained at his table during the fracas. There was a Colt revolver on the table near his hand and he casually flipped back the dark coat he wore to reveal the badge pinned to his vest. "It's over in this town. Maybe we ain't much of a town, but we don't need a lot of crazy balloonists starting trouble here. Get what you came for and get out of town— without any more trouble or I'll lock the whole damn bunch of you up."

Chambers' men slowly holstered their weapons. Chambers, holding his wrist, backed away from the table. Glancing again at the lawman he leaned forward and hissed at Jessica, "You got lucky this time, all of you. This time. But don't think this is close to being over, lady. It's just the beginning."

Chapter 7

The barber seemed to know what he was doing, but he wasn't big on communication. He grumbled and fussed as he brought out his carbolic, scissors, tape, and gauze. Jessica and Ki waited with Dana as the little man worked him over.

"What about Chambers?" she asked.

"His attitude—it's pretty clear that he thinks we were trying to sabotage him, and he's mad."

"Was he mad enough to strike back a couple of days ago?"

"Maybe. Maybe Gregor's behind it all. No telling where he is now. He could still be on the desert, or miles ahead of us."

Dana grunted as the barber soaked his wound with carbolic. Jessica looked up and smiled. "You're tough, remember?"

"Did I say that—shooting off my mouth again! Ouch! Dammit, that hurts."

The barber pointed at a faded sign, which said "No Profanity," and continued daubing at the wound.

"Dan Altmore," Jessica said. No one knew what she meant. "At the Lexington Hotel where Father and I stayed in Houston. There was a man named Dan Altmore who had been kicked by a horse. He bought some crutches from a traveling salesman and settled in at the Lexington to rest. One day he hobbled out of his room and a crutch snapped. He tumbled down the stairs, landed on his head, broke his right wrist—and got arrested for using profanity by the sheriff, who happened to be sitting at the foot of the stairs."

The barber had decided to take a few stitches despite Dana's vigorous objections. When he was finished there were beads of sweat on Cadge's forehead. "But didn't use any goddamned profanity," he congratulated himself.

The barber taped him up and helped him to his feet. When they paid him he looked the coin over carefully and tucked it away. Outside it was hot, nearly a hundred, Jessica guessed, although it was still early.

Crossing to the general store they found Professor Sperry making arrangements to have a fifty-gallon drum of kerosene delivered to the balloon. Melinda had an assortment of tinned goods on the counter.

"I don't dare serve stew again," she said with a laugh.

"Has Chambers been around?" Cadge Dana asked.

"No, no sign of him. Maybe the marshal scared him off."

"He doesn't seem to be the kind who scares easily," Dana said. "How soon can we get off the ground and out of this place?"

"An hour. If everyone's up to it," the professor said.

"If everyone's thinking the same way I am," Cadge replied, "we'd rather be back in the air than waiting around until Chambers gets another idea."

"Ki?" Melinda asked. "What do you think? We all need rest, you more than the rest of us."

"Let's go," Ki said. "I don't work on board. There's plenty of time to rest."

The general store clerk sent the kerosene and a coil of light wire over in a freight wagon. The kids, fewer of them, were still hanging around. So was Art Cortez.

Melinda, Dana, and Ki got busy trying to wire the battered gondola together. It wasn't pretty when they got done, but at least the thing would hold together. The burner started with its familiar pop and the balloon started to reinflate.

"Last chance, Cortez," Eric told him. "Better start walking."

"Maybe I've changed my mind."

"Nobody invited you on board. Why don't you just leave?" Eric was in the smaller man's face now, his fists bunched.

"Knock it off, Eric," Dana said.

"Who's going to stop me? You? We gave this little bastard a ride out of the mountains, didn't we? Why's he want to stick now? Get rid of him, the sooner the better."

"Professor?" Dana said. "What about Cortez? He says he wants to stay with us now."

"He can go or stay as he pleases. We can use another man."

"He goes!" Eric said. He put his hand in Cortez's face and shoved. The little man staggered backward, hit the rail, and sagged to the deck. Eric moved in on him.

"You heard me. Haven't you got the message yet, Cortez?"

"I think," Ki put in quietly, "that the professor has already made the decision." He helped Cortez to his feet and managed to step in between the two men at the same time. "Yes?"

Eric looked as if he was going to try it, but he had seen enough of Ki's work to lack that sort of confidence. He spun and walked away, driving his fist against the palm of his hand.

"There's the one who ought to go," Dana said.

The balloon was nearly round now, the silk moving with a slow rippling motion as it neared full inflation. They rose slowly into the cloudless sky, the children waving, racing after them, growing smaller and smaller. None of them was sorry to be leaving Wallace.

Chambers was still on the ground, his balloon still deflated. "Wonder what his problem was," Dana said. "I wish we'd had the chance to talk to the man and find out what happened."

The desert was flat and white, gleaming in the bright sunlight. Far ahead was a row of low mountains, untimbered, flood-cut. The balloon sailed on easily. Cortez kept out of everybody's way. Jessica decided to try sleeping in the cabin while the air was calm.

"There he is," Cadge said, pointing out the big balloon ahead of them. "Tyler Gregor's managed to keep out of trouble, it seems."

"It looks like we've both got trouble," Ki said.

"What do you mean?"

"Off to the north. Look at that wall of dust."

Dana turned around and looked across the desert. A wall of dark cloud was moving toward them from the north. "What is it, a sandstorm?"

"That's right."

69

"We should be able to outrun it, shouldn't we?"

Ki just shook his head. He didn't know, but he knew it was trouble if they didn't. He had seen men smothered by sand-storms, others blinded. Whether they could get above it or beyond it he couldn't say. They would just have to wait and hope.

Hoping didn't help. An hour later wind-shipped particles of sand stung their faces and their exposed flesh. The sand-storm was a howling, whistling black wall reaching from the desert floor to well above them.

It hit hard and the world went dark. The balloon tossed crazily. Ki had his scarf over his face and was knotting his safety line to the rail. There was nothing much he could do but crouch down and lower his head. Melinda sat beside him, and he put his arm around her as the hot, lashing storm battered the balloon.

They held on—that was all there was to do—and tried to protect their faces. The balloon rose and fell, spun and jerked savagely as the storm continued for hour after hour, blotting out the sun, erasing all other sounds but its howl.

When it finally ended just before sunset they rose wearily, frosted with sand, eyes burning, ears plugged with it.

"Jesus," Cadge Dana muttered, yanking down his scarf. "Well, at least we made it."

The balloon was intact, everyone was safe—but the dam-age the sandstorm had caused was worse than they had thought at first. The professor walked over to them, holding a round brass object in his hand.

"The compass," he said. "Ruined. Clogged with sand."

"Are we off course?" Dana asked.

"We must be a hundred miles off course. Don't ask me in which direction, though."

In all directions the desert stretched out endlessly. There were the mountains they had seen earlier, but they didn't look the same, and after an hour of going over her charts Melinda shrugged helplessly.

"I really can't tell where we are."

"Ki?" Jessica asked.

"Nothing from up here looks like it does from the ground.

70

It's possible that we've traveled this country before, but I can't recognize it."

"What's the difference?" Cadge Dana asked. "We know we want to go east.. We can figure that out."

"The difference in the end will be between fourteen-thousand-foot Rocky Mountain peaks and a safe passage through," Melinda told him.

"For now, we can't do anything but drift," Professor Sperry said. "Hope that the winds know more about where they are going than we do."

"Gregor's balloon is well out of sight," Jessica said.

"There's a chance he went down."

"Chambers was probably still on the ground. The odds are he's on a truer course than we are."

Cortez, apparently whipped, just stood at the rail and watched the desert flow by. Eric and the professor watched the burner. Melinda studied her charts. The rest of them weren't much use, and they knew it.

"You getting your story, Cadge?" Jessica asked.

"Part of it," he answered, leaning against the rail with his elbows. His blond hair lifted in the wind.

"What's bothering you?" she asked. She knew there was something on the man's mind.

"Just wondering if they'll let me print the story."

"Who? Your editors?"

"No—Gregor and Chambers." Cadge Dana smiled crookedly. "You really think they want the whole story of this race published?"

"I suppose not. Is that all there is to it, Cadge?"

He smiled crookedly again and looked to the east, toward the mountains. "Maybe not, but it's a consideration, isn't it? They really can't afford to let this balloon get through now, not if they can help it. Because one of those crews is a pack of murderers."

"He's right," Ki said later as he and Jessica sat alone in the cabin talking. "They can't let the whole story come out. And it doesn't just mean taking care of Dana—all of us know what has happened here."

"We're marked."

71

"That's right. Marked for death. You, me, Cadge, Eric, Melinda, and the professor."

"You left out Cortez."

"We're not quite sure about him yet, are we?" Ki replied with a smile.

There was a shout out on deck. It sounded like Eric. Jessie and Ki looked at each other, rose, and rushed out of the cabin.

It was no cooler outside than it had been hours earlier. Still the hot winds blew, still the white sun beat down. It was indeed Eric who had yelled. They saw immediately what had brought the shout from his throat.

There it was, no more than a quarter-mile ahead. The big black-and-white-striped balloon of Tyler Gregor.

"We're not so far off course after all," Jessica said.

Melinda answered, "Unless they're as lost as we are."

"The wind only blows one way," Eric said in his usual caustic tone.

"We seem to be gaining on them," Ki noticed.

"I don't doubt it. We've overboarded a lot of weight since the Sierra Nevadas."

The balloons drew nearer together. It was the first time since the race began that they had been close enough to see human beings on the gondola of the Gregor balloon. They were small, indistinct figures, like the human beings they had seen on the ground from altitude, hardly real, unsubstantial.

They suddenly got a lot more substantial.

The Winchesters opened up and bullets flew across the deck of Sperry's airship. Whining off metalwork, bullets angled off into the sky beyond them. Ki, in a crouch, went to the cabin for his rifle while Jessica tried to answer the fire from the black-and-white balloon with her sidearm.

Spinning .44-40 slugs pierced the gondola's fragile bodywork and punctured the balloon. Moving to the rail with his rifle, Ki levered through a half dozen rounds of ammunition. They could see the riflemen aboard Gregor's balloon duck, and in a minute the black-and-white craft veered away from them.

It was too late for Art Cortez. He stood upright, blood from his chest leaking through his clutching fingers. He turned angrily to Eric and said, "Dammit! I told you I wasn't one of 'em. I should have walked . . ."

Then Cortez slumped to the deck of the gondola and lay twitching for a few minutes before he died.

"Well," Dana said, "it's a war now, isn't it?"

"Yes," Ki agreed. "Any doubts we might have held on to are gone."

Melinda was incredulous, stunned. "I can't believe it! I can't understand how anyone could kill for this prize!"

"A lot of bank robbers get away with less than fifty thousand dollars," Jessica pointed out. "Anyway, we know who the enemy is now."

"Who?" Dana scoffed. "Chambers threatens to murder us, Tyler Gregor does just that—he killed one of us, and we're lucky it wasn't more than one."

"Anything in the air," Ki said, "is an enemy. I think we ought to look at it that way."

"Savages," Professor Sperry said passionately. "The chance we have here for science! Their greed is ruining everything."

"Father . . . we could quit. We could simply quit."

"No." The scientist was too stubborn for that. "Never."

"What do we do with *him?*" Eric asked, nodding at Art Cortez's body.

"There's not much choice," Ki said, looking at the rail.

They picked the body up and rolled it over, watching briefly as Cortez floated toward the desert floor. Melinda turned away. It wasn't her idea of being civilized.

It wasn't Ki's either, but there was no other way. Slowly they dispersed. Sperry and Eric went back to their burner as the balloon drifted on toward the low dark mountains beyond the desert. They could no longer see the black-and-white balloon. Gregor's ship had crested the first line of hills already and lost itself in the tangle of canyons and ridges beyond.

"I guess you saw them," Jessica said to Ki, and he nodded.

Yes, he too had seen the orange-and-blue balloon coming up behind them. Chambers was back in the race.

"It's a frustrating sort of war," Jessica said, "the only one we've been in where we can't just strike back, get your hands

73

on them and make *them* pay a little."

"That time will come, Jessica," Ki said. He was grim. "I promise you that time will come—and I will get my hands on these killers."

"I hope you're not planning on leaving me out of it," Jessica said. Ki smiled, touched her shoulder once, gently, and then shook his head.

They crested the first row of hills themselves and followed a shallow canyon eastward. The hills had nothing but nopal cactus and scattered chaparral growing on them. They ran into updrafts again—nothing serious, although once or twice people were thrown to the deck.

Jessica had gotten past the point where she could enjoy the effortless flight of the balloon over hundreds of miles of empty country. She was long past that. The sky was filled with killers.

Ki was deep in thought, and Jessie nudged him with her elbow. "What are you thinking about?"

"Getting my hands on them," he answered simply.

"How? Sprout wings?"

"They touch down every night, don't they? If a person could find Gregor on the ground, he could do some damage."

"Yes, and it would be nearly impossible to find him after dark, wouldn't it?"

Ki nodded. It would be tough. He would have fifty miles in any direction to consider—but if they could somehow locate the camp of the killers . . . They owed those men a little something and it was time to start paying them back.

Ki spent the rest of the afternoon forward with the brass-bound telescope to his eye, searching for that big black-and-white aircraft of Tyler Gregor's.

"Any luck?" Dana asked.

Ki put the telescope down and glanced at the blond reporter. "Not yet, but we know they're up there, don't we?"

"Jessica wants to go, Ki, if you decide to make any sort of attack. Don't let her."

Ki glanced over his shoulder. Jessica, hair trailing in the wind, was helping Melinda splice a frayed line.

"I don't intend to," he promised Dana.

"I wish I was up to it," Cadge said with some anger.

"You're not. I will do better alone—assuming we can find them at all. I want Sperry to set down as close to them as possible."

"Dangerous."

"So is getting sniped at. Ask Cortez."

"We'll have to fly late. Gregor's been putting down after dark every night."

Ki shrugged. "I don't think he will in this country. We'll just have to wait and see."

"Chambers is catching up with us, you know."

"Yes, I saw him."

Ki continued to scan the horizon. The sun was going down behind them, the deeper shadows collecting in the folds of the hills. Sperry was growing nervous. From time to time he came down to ask Ki if it wasn't all right to set down.

Ki's answer was invariable. "Not yet."

But it looked like they were going to have to do just that very soon. Dusky light cast a huge shadow in the balloon's shape against the dark, convoluted hills. There was only a little deep purple light left in the western sky.

Then he spotted it.

His heart gave one exultant leap as the professor's balloon struggled up and over one last hogback ridge. Nestled in a hidden valley just below them was the balloon. Ki thought he saw someone point up at them, or perhaps shoulder a rifle, but by then they were over the ridge and Ki was shouting, "Put it down! Here. The first spot over the ridge!"

Dana reminded Ki, "If you can find them, they can find us."

"That's why I want you to take off again," Ki answered, closing the telescope.

"Do *what?*"

Jessica had come up to listen, and she too thought Ki had lost his mind. "If we take off again, Ki, where does that leave you?"

"Right where I want to be," the *te* master answered, handing the telescope to Cadge.

They had already started to descend. Eric was cussing

something or perhaps everything. Melinda, in a coat now, stood beside Ki looking up at him with worried blue eyes.

"Ki, you'll never be able to find us in the darkness. I don't like any part of this. You'll get yourself killed, and if you fail at that, you'll get yourself lost. Reconsider it!"

"I have been considering it all day," Ki answered. "Our lives are at stake—yours, Jessica's. And I happen to care about you ladies. We can't fight in the sky. I'm going to have to go after them down on the ground. It's stop them now or let them pick us off one at a time. I don't intend to let that happen."

"But, Ki," Dana said. "How in hell do you intend to find us?"

Ki looked at the sky. "You won't be able to fly much farther. Five miles? Downwind. I'll follow the wind back, and with any luck I'll find you. There's been a moon. Just before sunrise build a fire to bring me in the rest of the way."

"And if you're not there at sunrise, an hour after sunrise, *two?*" Melinda said almost frantically.

"In that case," Ki said, "common sense dictates that I won't be back and that you should continue the race without me."

The balloon touched ground and Ki leaped over the rail, landing roughly on the rock-strewn earth of the hillside. He rose, dusted his knees, and watched as the balloon began to lift again, sailing through the dusk toward farther, darker hills.

Ki lifted a hand to those watching from the rail of the gondola and then looked upward to the hogback ridge in front of him. It was going to be a bad climb in the near darkness, but it had to be done, and so he started upward.

It was completely dark by the time he crested the ridge and sat catching his breath by starlight. The moon had not yet risen, and that was both bad and good. Ki could barely make out a way down the hogback. He looked forward to more skinned knees and hands.

The raiders could look forward to worse than that, much worse. Out of the dark of the mountainside they would never see Ki coming.

Ki glanced over his shoulder, making sure he had his bearings for later, and then started down the slope toward the campfire he had spotted below. It glowed like a beacon in the night.

Tyler Gregor would have reason to regret building that campfire before the night was over.

Chapter 8

Ki crept down the slope, his mind on his offensive. His ultimate purpose was, of course, to put Gregor out of the race. With him stranded in these hills he couldn't work any more mischief. What happened to him after that Ki didn't care particularly. Cadge Dana would write up the events of the race and there would be no room in San Francisco for Tyler Gregor. If the law wanted to track him down, then they could.

Ki just wanted to keep his people safe.

He didn't expect to have it happen without bloodshed. Gregor and his men had already shown themselves willing to kill.

Squatting on the ledge, his hand around his wrist, Ki scanned the valley below, trying to work out his approach. He could see the big striped balloon, half inflated, see a man move in front of the fire from time to time. Once he heard a distance-muted laugh.

It wasn't going to be easy.

To move into an armed camp alone never was, never would be. Then he would have to make his escape over the hills. The trick was to do the maximum damage with the maximum speed and get the hell out of there.

Maximum damage. The burner, if he could get to it somehow. Out of commission, it would keep Gregor grounded. If not—somehow destroy the balloon fabric itself. Fire, maybe? Maybe.

A dull glow like the wink of a glittering eye. Ki's eyes narrowed as he glanced that way, northward. Then slowly he smiled. It had to be, must be, Walt Chambers' camp.

Better and better.

The two camps weren't more than a mile apart, but they were cut off from each other's view by a ragged, broken ridge.

Why fight them at all? Ki asked himself. Let them do it to each other.

Ki climbed down the rest of the way with higher expectations. By the time he reached the cool canyon bottom he was sure it would work.

He worked his way around Gregor's camp and started toward the other campfire. Ki used the high ground where he could, making his way across the nearly brushless hillsides until he was above the fire Walt Chambers' crew had started.

He spent some time studying the camp, looking for sentries. Three men had already rolled up in their beds near the fire. The sole guard that Ki saw was leaning against the small, rectangular gondola of the balloon, rifle butt on the ground, muzzle in his hands.

Satisfied, Ki went down.

He slid down a shallow gully and came up onto the flat ground from behind the gondola. Moving in a crouch, he slipped around the corner of the guard's post and took a quick look. The man with the rifle was in the same position.

In a moment he wouldn't be.

The guard yawned, and suddenly a hand clapped over his mouth. He struggled to get free but talonlike fingers were jammed into the bundle of nerves beside his neck. The pain was paralyzing, and no matter how he struggled he couldn't shake free. His rifle dropped to the ground and he followed. Ki picked up the rifle and slipped out of the camp.

The rifle was a good one, a Winchester needle gun with a seventeen-shot capacity. Ki started burning up some of those rounds. He couldn't see the burner, but he had an idea where it had to be. From a kneeling position, he opened up.

A bullet whined satisfyingly off metal and the Chambers crew rolled from their beds with a shout. Ki put a round in the dust at one man's feet and another over their heads, then got back to work on the balloon.

Three more shots were fired at the burner, two of them

whining off iron and brass. Ki lifted his sights then to the balloon, but he was running out of time as answering fire began to pepper the earth near his position.

Ki took to his heels. Returning to the gulley he again achieved higher ground. He paused on the path to wait for his pursuit. He didn't want to make it too hard for them.

They seemed to be lost already, or perhaps they were just reluctant to come ahead. Ki fired two shots randomly and waited another minute to make sure they knew which direction he had taken.

Then, smiling with grim satisfaction, he loped along the hillside toward Tyler Gregor's camp, pausing at intervals to let his pursuers catch up. Ki glanced to the far hills and saw the sky paling. The moon would be rising soon; he wanted this done with before that happened.

In the darkness no one knew what was happening, who was shooting or where their targets were. That was just the way Ki wanted it. The Gregor camp would be alert now. They would have heard the shots and snatched up their own weapons. That, too, was just the way Ki wanted things.

A man popped up suddenly in front of Ki, astonished to find the dark figure bearing down on him. He reached for a holstered Colt but never got it out of leather. Ki was all over him, knocking him to the earth with a knee to the solar plexus, finishing him with a short, chopping blow to the neck. Ki rose, looked over his shoulder, and ran on.

He found a hillside position, cocked his rifle, and waited. At the moment the Chambers crew burst angrily over the last ridge, Ki opened fire on Gregor's camp.

Ki's first shot brought a yelp of pain from a man who dragged himself away on one good leg. Ki's shot was answered immediately by a hail of bullets from below.

Chambers' crew, charging over the ridge and downslope, answered the gunfire immediately.

With both crews engaged in the firefight Ki was free to snipe at the balloon. Rifle shots roared in his ears, flame stabbed from gun muzzles below and behind him. He carefully used his last few minutes, taking deliberate aim at the

80

vital burner of Gregor's balloon. He couldn't be sure he hit it. The gunfight continued furiously, men falling on both sides as Gregor charged down the hill and was repulsed, taking up a position behind a stand of rocks to continue the attack.

Ki's hammer fell on an empty chamber and he placed the rifle aside. Circling wide of the camp he picked up his trail, and by the light of the moon started walking eastward.

It hadn't been a complete victory, perhaps, but Ki was pleased with his night's work. Let the thugs kill each other off, destroy each others' balloons. The gunshots continued for almost an hour until Ki was over the hills and well on his way.

There was no way on earth he was going to find the camp at night, and so he found himself a sheltered hollow and sat down, looping his arms around his knees, to watch the moon rise.

When the moon was fading and dawn beginning to glow in the east, Ki rose again and moved on. From the top of a cone-shaped, barren hill he picked out the dully shining distant fire and went ahead more rapidly.

In two hours he was in Doctor Sperry's camp, exhausted but happy. Melinda was the first one to reach him, and she hugged him tightly, looking up into his dusty face.

"You scared me, Mister," she said, touching his cheek.

"Any luck?" Jessica wanted to know.

"Some. We'll talk about it later. For now, let's get in the air as quickly as possible, right?"

The balloon rose into the face of the dawn sun. Ki sat on the deck of the gondola and related what he had done. "They had themselves a decent firefight. I know a couple of them are out of action, and hope the balloons are. I'm almost sure I eliminated Chambers' burner."

"They could have a spare."

"They could, but that will take time to refit. I think we've slowed them down a little and that's the main thing—to get far enough ahead so that we don't have to worry about what they might pull next."

"I wish I'd been there," Cadge said.

"You're not in shape for that kind of work," Jessica said.

"I heal fast. I'm about ready to pull these bandages off." He mused, "That would have made good reading for the *Post* subscribers."

"Haven't you got enough grist for that particular mill by now?" Jessie asked.

"Oh, sure. I have enough, but I always like to get the whole story, Jessica. That's the point in reporting, isn't it? To get the complete story. That's why I'm here—that's what I mean to do." With that, Dana turned and left, whistling softly to himself as they sailed on over the dust-colored hills toward the more menacing range of blue mountains beyond.

"He still isn't saying everything he knows," Ki commented. "I thought you were going to see what you could get out of him."

Jessica laughed. "That didn't work out exactly as planned."

Ki only lifted an eyebrow. He could see the look in Jessie's eyes as she followed Cadge's progress down the narrow deck.

Melinda was in a triumphant mood as she came and sat down in front of Ki, cross-legged on the deck. She tossed back her long, loose red hair and said, "Congratulate me. I'm a genius."

"Yes?"

"The compass!" She held it up for them to marvel at. At Ki's nod she complained, "No one appreciates a genius. I got the sand out, refloated the needle and the darn thing's actually working."

"How do you know it's working?" Ki asked quietly.

"Well . . . it is, that's all. There's north, see. Since the sun is over there, it's obviously working!"

Ki grinned. "Just teasing, Melinda. I suppose mechanical geniuses can't take much kidding either."

"The important thing is that it keeps working. Eric will have to bolt it up to the stand again, and we'll keep an eye on it."

"Eric's been quiet lately—for Eric," Jessica said.

"He's been quiet, but didn't you see him last night?" Melinda asked.

"Did I see him? Of course . . . When do you mean, Melinda?" Jessica asked in puzzlement.

"When he was standing over your bed staring at you. I think with Ki gone he was starting to get funny ideas. I lobbed a rock at his back and he went away."

"I don't like that," Ki said.

"It doesn't bother me," Jessica said confidently. "I can handle Eric if it comes to that."

"Maybe," Ki answered. He had taught Jessica a trick or two and she could hold her own with most men who had no idea of what they were walking into, but Eric was a big man, very big. "All the same, I'll try to keep a better eye on him."

"You can hardly keep your eyes open just now," Melinda said, rising with her prized compass, dusting off the seat of her jeans. "You'd better try to get some sleep in the cabin."

Ki nodded obediently. There was no pretending that he didn't need sleep, and badly. He had trouble getting to his feet. By the time he had been stretched out on the cabin floor with a single blanket over him for three minutes, he was sound asleep.

No one woke him up to tell him about the problem.

Jessica saw it first, or rather felt it. Her foot slipped on the deck, and looking down, she saw a small, indistinct smear. She put her finger to it and smelled it.

"Cadge?"

"What is it?"

Jessica was bent over, following a narrow liquid trail into the main storage compartment.

By the time Dana followed her in she had found the trouble. She turned, hands on hips, and muttered a word Cadge didn't think she knew.

"Those snipers did more damage than we thought," Jessica said, angrily pushing at her hair with her fingertips.

"What do you mean?"

"The kerosene drum, Cadge. Take a look. Three rounds through it. It's been seeping out and no one saw it." She tilted the fifty-gallon drum and shook it. If it had more than five gallons of fuel left in it she would be surprised.

"Now what do we do?" Dana asked.

83

"Tell Sperry and hope we can find some other little town out here somewhere before the burner runs dry and we go down to stay."

"Nothing to it," Cadge said, frowning. "There's probably three or four towns within five hundred miles of us."

"We'll have to see if Melinda can find one on her charts."

"What are the odds of finding kerosene, assuming we do find some busted mining camp or four-corner cowtown?"

Jessica didn't answer. The odds were about as good as Cadge figured they were, ranging from poor to worse. She went up to find Professor Sperry and give him the bad news.

There was nothing on the charts, just nothing. Melinda, on hands and knees, the edges of her chart weighted down with hardware, pored over the bundle of charts she had and found nothing.

"What's this then?" Cadge asked, pointing out a circle within a circle which seemed to indicate a settlement.

"Ghost town, Cadge," the redhead told him. "Silver Springs? I've never heard of it."

"Seems to ring a bell somewhere in the back of my mind," Jessica told them. "Why, I don't recall. A typical boom camp, I imagine. The ore is there, and then when it's stripped out, there's no reason for remaining."

"No help," Melinda said. "That is just no help at all."

"Maybe there's still someone there," Cadge said. "Maybe they've left some goods behind—kerosene for example."

"You're optimistic today."

"We don't seem to have much choice," Cadge said as Melinda let her charts roll up again and tucked them away in their leather cannister. "Where else is there?"

"Nowhere." Jessica bit at her lower lip. Maybe . . . It was a long shot, but then miners did need kerosene for their lamps, didn't they? That or coal oil. Why take half a drum of kerosene away when the town was abandoned? She and Melinda looked at each other. The professor's daughter shrugged.

"The longest of long shots," Melinda decided.

"Yes," Jessica Starbuck agreed. "But Cadge has put his finger on it, hasn't he? Where else is there?"

They discussed matters with Sperry. He had as much confidence in the notion as the rest of them did, but in the end he had to agree with them—it was set down in Silver Springs and hope for the best or simply fall to the ground when the burner, its fuel exhausted, failed.

Eric, in a foul temper, kept his mouth shut, but he didn't keep his eyes off Jessica. Cadge didn't like it, but decided to keep his own mouth shut for the time being.

There was a single bright spot in their situation, and Jessica mentioned it. "At least we're alone in the sky. Ki seems to have managed to take out the opposition."

It was true. They had seen nothing in the clear blue skies all day—no following balloons, no angry snipers.

Cadge Dana said, "It seems now that they took us out first."

He might have been right, Jessica decided. They floated on for mile after endless mile, their course altered to Melinda's calculation based on her possibly inaccurate charts and probably unreliable compass.

Their new tack took them into wooded hills. There was much pine and scattered cedar and aspen below them now, long meadows, some barren, many golden with grass. They spotted a large elk herd which ran as they came in low over the valley, and once they saw an ambling black bear with two cubs.

Ki, awake if not fully alert, came on deck and was told what was happening. He had other misgivings as well.

Looking to the Rocky Mountains, approaching far too quickly, he wondered aloud, "How are we going to get over those giants, fuel or none?"

"If—*when* we do get over them," Melinda said, quickly correcting herself, "why, the race is practically won. The country grows flatter, the wind currents more reliable. There will be more towns in case of trouble—"

"When," Ki smiled, "and *if.*"

They didn't see the ghost town until they were almost past it. Silver Springs, gray, half hidden by timber, was perched on a hillside that showed signs of hydraulic or strip mining. Above the town, the mountain, which sat sat at something around six thousand feet, was rutted by runoff, naked of timber. An open shaft was visible halfway up the slope. No living thing was to be seen in the town itself.

"Bad gamble," Cadge muttered.

"We've got two gallons of fuel left," Melinda said. "There'd better be something to burn here."

"The town," Cadge replied caustically.

Maybe that was the fate the town deserved and had so far avoided. After tying down, they explored Silver Springs, finding streets filled with weeds and abandoned wagons. There was a hardware store with a twisted awning half fallen down over a sagging porch; four empty, cobwebbed saloons; a hotel with a moldy carpet and broken windows; and a handful of smaller buildings that couldn't be identified but were in general disrepair, rat-infested, and in one case roofless.

"And we're supposed to find fuel here?" Eric complained.

"We can try." It hadn't gotten dark yet, but glancing at the sky, Ki knew it wouldn't be long in the shadow of the mountains. "We'll try the businesses first and then, if we have no luck, maybe the mines. They had to be burning something. I spotted a kerosene lamp in the hotel."

"Terrific," Eric muttered. "We can empty all the lamps in town into a barrel and use that as fuel."

"If we have to," Professor Sperry said, "that is exactly what we will do."

"We won't do much looking around tonight," Dana said. "Jessica and I will get the blankets from the gondola. Maybe the rest of you can find something worth sleeping on in the hotel in the meantime."

Ki looked again to the skies and nodded. "That's about all we can do. Maybe there *is* enough fuel in those hotel lamps to give us some illumination."

"Bring some grub," Eric said. Cadge looked back at him and nodded. Then he and Jessica took off through the sundown light toward the balloon while the others returned to the hotel they had briefly explored.

Pack rats and owls had used the place to make their nests, and as they returned in near darkness a snake slithered away underfoot. The third lantern they tried had enough residual kerosene to come to life when Ki touched a match to the flat woven wick.

They had a better look around then.

The carpet was mildewed, stained. The walls showed signs of leaking water—and a couple of bullet holes. The first few rooms they looked into weren't promising. Chewed blankets, mildewed mattresses, broken furniture. Upstairs, however, things were different. The blankets had to go, but the mattresses were usable, even a few of the pillows. They were clean enough for one night although Melinda went hunting for a broom.

"These lamps along the hallway seem to have kerosene in them," Sperry announced.

"Good, we can use a few more," Ki answered. "After a while I'm taking another look through that storeroom. They must have had a stock somewhere."

Cadge and Jessica had returned with their bedrolls and Melinda had found something that looked as if it might once have been a broom. Eric, standing at the hall window, was grunting as he ate something out of a tin can.

Ki returned to the cellar storeroom they had looked through earlier and gave it a better look. Broken, empty crates made up most of the litter there. A few tin cans, a rusting set of iron pots, jugs smashed to shards, a lot of rags.

No kerosene.

They would have to hope that one of the mine sites proved out. Otherwise they were in for failure—and a hell of a long hike out. Ki looked around once more, walked to the door on the back alley, and stepped into the night air. The stars were bright. A few clouds floated high above the mountains. The alley, clotted with debris, offered no miraculous gifts, although Ki, not wanting to miss a chance, kicked around in the litter for a while.

Lights were on upstairs when he went back in, blew out his own lamp, and went up.

"No luck?" Jessica asked.

Ki shook his head. "Everything worth taking seems to be gone. Still, I can't believe anyone would want a half-used drum of kerosene."

"We do," Jessica reminded him and Ki smiled, tilting his head. The lady, when she was right, was right.

"Are you going to eat?"

"I don't think so," Ki answered. "Tea would be good, but we have none. I'm going to bed—which room is mine?"

"I think number four," Jessica said with a wink. "It's the cleanest. I thought Melinda was going to polish that brass bed."

Ki put his lantern down and climbed the staircase. It was number four all right. Melinda was inside with a scarf around her head.

"Look what I found," she said breathlessly. At first Ki had no idea what it was. Small, brass, intricate. She held it up. "The key to the door. Use it, Ki," she said, and slipped from her dress.

Chapter 9

Ki locked the door and pocketed the key. He sat down on the bed as Melinda, naked and beautiful, stood before him. His hands ran up across her smooth, firm ass to her spine as his mouth met her soft abdomen.

Reaching up he found her breasts and cupped them. She smiled down, her hands covering his. "Lie back," she said.

Ki leaned back onto the mattress, feeling her fingers at the buttons of his jeans, at his belt buckle. She was humming under her breath, the tune indistinct, soothing.

Clumsily she tugged his trousers down over his hips. Ki sprang free and Melinda paused to cradle his love candle in both hands, to bend her head to it, her red hair spilling across his thighs and abdomen.

"Forgot . . ." she said, and returned to her task. Ki's slippers hit the floor, and then his pants. He tugged his shirt up and over and flung it aside as Melinda lifted herself onto the bed.

Naked, ivory-white, she looked down into Ki's face. Starlight fell through the window and the pale moon glow was faintly visible. She was over him, on her knees, and she bent her sweet moist mouth to his, her kiss lingering, her tongue finding his as her hand again wrapped around his solid shaft.

Melinda threw her leg over Ki and from a kneeling position she inched forward, tucking the head of his erection into her soft body. She swayed against him, bending low for an occasional kiss. Her breasts moved from side to side and Ki brushed their taut nipples with the palms of his hands at each pendulum stroke.

Melinda lifted her hips and slowly settled, throwing back her head with pleasure as she did so. She wriggled against Ki contentedly and then lifted herself again so that only the very tip of him was within her.

"Do you like it, Ki?"

"What do you think?"

"Is it very good, Ki?" she asked teasingly, settling to the hilt once again. "I want you to fill me up. Feel how damp I am already. Touch me there once."

"You're asking for it, lady," Ki said as he reached between Melinda's sleek thighs to touch the damp softness where he entered her.

She laughed. "That's right. I'm asking for it, do it, Ki, please?"

Ki arched his back slightly, driving it in even deeper. Melinda bent low to kiss his mouth greedily as he lifted her again, his lean hard body bucking against hers. Ki gripped her neck and held her mouth to his as he continued to thrust deeply.

"Please, Ki," Melinda gasped, and he came, fountaining inside of her as she reached a furious orgasm, writhing, clutching at him, sitting up and then falling against him, reaching between her own legs to touch his hardness.

"What was the big hurry?" Ki asked as he stroked her hair and soft shoulders.

"I wanted it once—we've got all night. Later we can take our time, nice and easy."

"You remember the last time we thought that," Ki said, kissing the lobe of her ear.

"Back there? That man with the axe? Yes, but . . ."

Ki had never laid claim to being prescient, but there must have been something in the back of his mind, something his concentration in other areas hadn't allowed him to focus on. As he again started to slowly move against Melinda, a crack and a violent curse resounded in the hallway.

"No!" Melinda wailed as he slipped from her and rolled to his feet. "Is it Gregor?"

Ki shook his head. He didn't know—but who else could it be? He threw his vest on and found the door key, opening it as another crash echoed down the hallway. Behind him Melinda was hastily dressing. He motioned for her to stay in the room, and then slipped into the lantern-lit hallway.

He was in time to see Eric go down on the seat of his pants and an infuriated, bandaged, bare-chested Cadge Dana moving in on him, both fists clenched.

"Get up you son of a bitch, I'm not done with you."

Glancing up the hall Ki saw the professor, wearing bifocals low on his nose, his face astonished. Jessica, a blanket around her shoulders, was standing in the doorway of her room.

Eric roared and launched himself at Dana. A stiff right stopped him in his tracks. Eric kicked at Cadge's groin but missed, his boot glancing off the reporter's thigh. Cadge began to show his boxing skills.

A left jab to Eric's nose started blood flowing from the red-headed mechanic's nostrils. A second jab off the mechanic's forehead stunned him and sent him staggering back.

"I'll kill you," Eric panted, although he didn't look like he was going to have much luck trying it with his bare hands.

"A goddamned Peeping Tom. Looking through ladies' keyholes." Cadge was still furious, his face the color of burned brick. He moved in on Eric again, giving him a right to the rib cage, followed by a hooking right to the ear. Eric pawed back, but for all of his size and obvious strength, he was overwhelmed by the attack of the newsman.

Eric tried to grab at Cadge's throat to throw him down, but Dana was too quick for him by far. Another left to the face sent Eric reeling. They had reached the end of the hallway now, though neither man seemed aware of it. Dana feinted with a left, which Eric tried to block, and then looped in a sledgehammer right and Eric went tumbling down the stairs, screaming like a woman, until he lay still at the foot of the stairway.

Cadge stood there watching, his chest rising and falling erratically. Blood leaked from beneath his bandages. Ki touched the newsman's arm gently.

"He's not going to get up again, Cadge. He's had enough. And so have you. You've torn your side open again."

"Yeah." Cadge grinned. "I can feel it, Ki."

"What happened anyway?"

"He was watching Jessica through the keyhole. I don't know what he had in mind, but I didn't like it and he tried to hit me with a chair. I think he did hit me with a chair," Cadge said, still grinning. He rubbed his head and winced.

"All right, go to bed," Ki said, slapping Cadge on the shoulder.

The *te* master went down the stairs to where Eric lay groaning. His neck wasn't broken and he seemed to be in one piece. He was breathing anyway. Ki crouched and lifted the man. Taking him to a filthy settee in the hotel lobby he placed him on it, shook his head, and went back upstairs.

The corridor was empty when he reached it again—and so, damn it all, was his room! There was only Melinda's scent and a memory to curl up with. Ki shrugged inwardly and stepped out of his trousers, crawling back into bed.

Morning was cool and damp. They were at six thousand feet and it seemed that it had misted a little overnight. Going downstairs Ki found the others in the kitchen, Melinda cooking over an iron stove while Jessica poured coffee.

"You're up late," Melinda said.

"You were gone early," he answered.

"I don't suppose *you've* seen Eric?" Jessica asked Ki.

"No. Is he gone?"

Jessica gave Ki a cup of coffee. "Took an hour to clean this place up enough to eat here," she said. "Yes, Eric's gone."

"Embarrassed. He'll be back. Where can he go?"

"That's true. Ki, do you still think there's a chance we can find kerosene?" Melinda asked.

"I *hope* we can. The miners would have used it, especially if they had machinery in here. I don't know what sort of camp Silver Springs was. All I can tell you is that we'll look."

"Father and Cadge are trying to scavenge what they can around town. They were waiting for you to get up before trying the mines."

Ki sipped at his coffee and watched the redhead work. It was a pleasant sight, he decided, as she went to tiptoes, bent over, moved gracefully around the room, humming that familiar nonsense tune.

Half an hour later Sperry and Cadge Dana came back, dusty and discouraged. They had a five-gallon can with them, which Cadge shook. The small lapping sound the kerosene made inside wasn't very encouraging.

"Every lamp in this town. Every single storeroom," Cadge said, sounding defeated. "That's what we got."

"We couldn't expect much more." Ki rose. "Shall we try the mine sites?"

Jessica asked, "No one has seen our friends in the sky?"

"No, maybe Ki solved that for us," Cadge said. "I kept looking up this morning, though."

"Let's start looking," Ki said. "It won't do us any good to have Chambers and Gregor out of this if we're out ourselves. If worse comes to worst, professor, with that little kerosene you've collected and what we have in the drum, could we clear the mountains?"

Sperry shook his head. "I wouldn't attempt it, Ki. We could come down rather nastily unless everything went exactly right."

"I see. All right." Ki sucked in a breath. "Let's hope there's some luck left in the world, then."

Outside, it was gray and windy. The temperature was hovering around forty degrees, but the wind made it feel much colder, blasting into their faces as they climbed the denuded slope toward the mineshaft they had seen earlier.

"We could split up," Jessica suggested. "There are probably other mines around. Cadge?"

"I'll go with you," Dana said eagerly.

Cadge and Jessica split off and started through the timber to the west. Ki didn't find the climb up the old mining road particularly difficult, but they had to stop twice for the professor to catch his breath.

The second time, Eric came out of the woods and Ki tensed. He marched up to them, his face bruised and battered, rifle in his hands. "I'm sorry," the mechanic said. "It wasn't too bright. Am I still with you or do I hike out?"

Ki was a moment responding. "You're still with us if you can get that other business out of your mind."

"Nothing I'd rather forget," Eric said.

"All right then." The two men shook hands, and then Eric

93

offered his hand to Sperry who smiled, happy to have his team back together.

Eric said, "I checked out a couple of small outbuildings downslope from here. Found an old pump, but there wasn't no fuel. I figured to go up to the main shaft next when I seen you coming."

"That'll save us a little time," Ki answered. He looked to the shifting skies as the professor rested. Almost unconsciously he scanned the western horizon, still searching for that big black-and-white-striped balloon.

When the professor was ready they went ahead another mile to the main shaft of a huge mine site. Cabins—offices, perhaps—sat in disrepair to the south, surrounded by litter, rusting tools, and broken machinery with frayed steel cables.

The wind whipped across the ridge more violently. It couldn't have been much of a place to work in the wintertime. Melinda, who had carried the lantern they would need in the shaft, lit it, and leaving Eric and the professor to scout around the buildings, she and Ki went into the mine proper.

The shaft had a hand-operated elevator, which Ki wouldn't have trusted with the weight of an underfed tomcat, and a disused, weather-splintered ladder, which he placed in the pit and climbed down, bracing it for Melinda.

"Now where?" Melinda asked. She was shivering with the cold. The wind was cut some by the shaft, but not enough. Two tunnels led off in different directions. The floor of one of the shafts had been laid with rails, now badly rusted.

"Your choice," Ki said. He had no hope of finding kerosene deep inside the mine. Such supplies would normally be kept above ground, but they couldn't afford to leave any stone unturned.

Melinda nodded right and they went that way, the lantern casting a feeble yellow glow against the broken walls of the tunnel. They followed the steel rails deeper into the tunnel. The shaft was horizontal here, but now and then they found dangerous stopes, downward shafts, and cubbyholes cut into the walls. Each they examined dutifully, finding nothing at all.

Still Ki could see traces of silver in the rock—not worth mining, obviously, or someone would have kept at it. The rails dead-ended a hundred yards into the shaft.

They stood there watching the light play on a stack of poor ore and the pick-grooved walls. Melinda shrugged. "Try the other shaft, I guess. Unless . . . this shaft?" She was against him, the palm of her hand fitted against Ki's crotch. He kissed her and felt the stirrings of desire.

"I'd like to, you know," Ki said.

"But no?"

"But no. With regret."

"Such is life." Melinda smiled and kissed him again, deeply. "Mister, if I ever get you to St. Louis and a hotel with real sheets . . . look out."

"If we don't find some kerosene, unfortunately, we're going nowhere."

"I know," she sighed, her hand falling away. "Okay, let's try the other shaft."

They did, but they had no luck at all. Inside, there was a wooden storage shed, but only rusting tools and battered miners' hats rested there.

"You notice that though?" Ki asked, fingering one of the hats.

"What?"

"Those are kerosene lamps on the hats."

"Yes." Melinda wasn't feeling optimistic. "And so we reach the conclusion that they took it away with them when they left. Loaded it on the wagons and away! Why throw useful material away? Take it on to the next boom site."

Ki put the hat back. The woman, damn it, was probably right.

They returned to the head of the tunnel, their own lantern faltering now from lack of fuel, and climbed the ladder out of the deep pit.

Eric was waiting for them as they reached the top.

"Where the hell you been fooling around?" he snarled. And then for the first time since Ki had known him, he broke into a smile. "Look over there," the mechanic said, and Ki saw Professor Sperry standing beside a fifty-gallon, blue-painted drum.

"It's not—?"

95

"No, it ain't. It's coal oil," Eric told them as they walked that way, "but give me a little time to adjust the jets on the burner and it'll do the job. Not as clean-burning, but it'll do it. We're on our way."

By rigging two circular collars of rope that they found in the same storehouse, they were able to let the drum roll down the mine road. Ki and Eric managed the slack while gravity did all the work, except for the occasional braking and steering.

They met Jessica and Cadge a quarter of a mile down the road. Cadge tensed at the sight of Eric, but Ki told him, "It's all over, Dana. He told us that. Funny thing is, I believe him. Maybe he was just asking to have the stuffing kicked out of him, and now that it's done we can go on."

"Coal oil?" Jessica said, and Eric explained about the modifications to the burner, half of which Jessie understood. Nevertheless, Eric sounded confident, and Professor Sperry trusted his mechanic.

"It burns colder," Sperry said, "but it'll do. Eric can handle it."

"Then we're on our way again," Jessica said.

They rolled the drum all the way to town and up the main street toward the balloon. They were nearing the hotel again when they found out they weren't alone.

"Ki," Jessica Starbuck said. "Company."

Ki looked up from his work. *Again?* Had Tyler Gregor caught up to them again? But it wasn't Gregor and his mob. Six men on horses walked their animals up the street. They were a ragged-looking bunch, in dirty, long coats, patched trousers, wide-brimmed hats.

Ki stopped, wiped his hands on his jeans, and waited. All but one of the strangers were bearded. Their leader—or the man in front—had a tangled mat of black beard down his coat front. He wore an old tweed coat, which flapped against the flanks of the fine-looking, leggy roan he rode.

"Who the hell are they?" Dana asked.

"I suppose we'll find out in a minute," Jessica answered. Her hand rested on the butt of her .38 revolver, although what good it would do against half a dozen armed men she didn't know. Dana wasn't carrying a gun, nor was the professor, of course. Eric had his rifle slung over his shoulder. Ki was armed with *shuriken*, of course, but starting any trouble would get Melinda and the professor in the line of fire.

Jessica wondered why she assumed these men were up to no good—since that was exactly what she was assuming— but as they neared she knew she was right.

Half a dozen rough men riding far from the nearest community, their clothing ragged, their guns new and oiled, their horses the very best. Outlaws.

The horsemen reined up, and the leader, the one with the black beard hanging to his belly, said, "My name's Lavender. This is my town."

Dark, tiny eyes swept Jessica's party, lingering on her and then on Melinda.

Professor Sperry was apologetic. "We certainly didn't realize anyone lived in this town, let alone owned it. We apologize for intruding—in fact we were just going to collect our gear and leave."

A young, blond rider with his torn hat well back on his head said something to Lavender. The blond had blue eyes that seemed slightly crossed, too-full lips, and a pair of gunbelts at his waist.

"That's right. Ernie, here," Lavender said, "points out that you folks have something that belongs to us." He nodded toward the drum of fuel oil.

"But we got this from the mine up there . . ." Sperry said, pointing up the slope.

"Yeah, I know. Thing is," Lavender said, hooking one leg around his saddlehorn, "I own the mine too."

"You own just about everything, don't you?" Eric said aggressively. Lavender's eyes narrowed to lifeless black beads.

"That's right. I own about everything."

"Eric, please," Sperry said. "We didn't intend to take anyone's property, Mr. Lavender. From all indications the town and mine have long been deserted. We assumed . . ."

"Scavengers," the blond kid said. He cackled just a little as he said it. "Nothin' but scavengers combing over everything. Stealin' whatever takes their fancy."

"I've been trying to explain," Sperry went on. "Of course, if the coal oil is yours we would be more than happy to pay for it."

"All right," Lavender drawled, rubbing his whiskered cheek. Ki saw him turn and wink at the man behind him, the one with the eye patch. "I'll take fifty dollars for it."

"Fifty dollars!" Melinda exclaimed. Lavender let his eyes slide to her, moving across her body like a snake.

"That's including the fine for stealin'," Lavender said.

Eric was incensed, nearly out of control. "Now you're telling us you're the law here as well!"

"Sure, that's right, Red. I'm judge and jury. I'm also the marshal. This here's my posse."

"Oh for goodness sake," Sperry said in exasperation. "Eric, control yourself. If the man wants fifty dollars then we'll give him fifty dollars and be done with it."

"Did I say fifty?" Lavender asked. One of his men laughed out loud. "I meant a hundred."

"You said fifty," Melinda argued.

"I've reconsidered. Your fine was raised. Breaking and entering—I forgot that." His men laughed again. Ki eased nearer to Jessica, who glanced at him with concern. This was a bad situation and they both knew it.

"All right—a hundred," Sperry said, digging into his money belt as Lavender watched.

"How much have you got in that belt, Pappy?" Lavender asked.

"Don't worry, I have your hundred."

"Why don't you just hand up the belt. I'll make change for you," the outlaw leader said.

"I don't need you to make change," Sperry said irritably.

"Yeah, you do." Suddenly there was a Remington .41 revolver in Lavender's hand. It was cocked and aimed at Sperry's head. "Hand the belt up here."

"There's five hundred dollars in there," Sperry objected. Lavender took the belt and handed it to his cross-eyed sidekick.

"No there ain't," the outlaw said. "There ain't even a hundred in here, Lavender."

"Why you liar!" Sperry sputtered. "Give me back that—"

He reached for the belt and saw it snatched away. The cross-eyed kid kicked the professor in the chest and he collapsed to the street. Eric took a step forward, but all the outlaws had their weapons out now. Ki stood like a man frozen by the cold winds. Eric looked to the *te* master for help but got none. Ki just shook his head slightly.

"You people don't have enough money here to pay your fines," Lavender went on, his tone deeply mocking now. "I'm sorry but I'm gonna have to arrest you."

"Just arrest the ladies, Lavender," the man with the eye-patch said, getting a big laugh.

"I'll hold 'em all for now. Until their barrister shows up. You, Red, unsling that rifle. Lady," he said aiming his gun at Jessica Starbuck, "you unbuckle that weapon you're carrying." He half turned in his saddle. "A couple of you deputies take your prisoners here off to jail. Riz! Break out that whisky. I think maybe we'll have to adjourn to the courtroom over there and discuss what to do with these prisoners."

The man with the patch, Riz, said, "And who gets which one first." His eyes were on Jessica as he said it and he smiled a yellow, broken-toothed smile that chilled Jessica to the bone.

Two of the riders had swung down, and now, prodding Jessica with their rifles, pushing the others ahead of them, they made their way back to the hotel, kicked the door open, and went in.

The basement was a perfect makeshift "jail" and it was into that filthy hole they were placed, the door barred behind them, closing out all light.

There was nothing to do then but sit and wait. Wait until the judge was drunk and passed sentence and the jury carried out the verdict—outlaw-style.

Chapter 10

Eric was in an uproar. They couldn't see him in the darkness of the storage room, but they couldn't help hearing him.

"If you'd helped me, Ki—and you, Dana—we could've taken care of them."

"The three of us," Cadge answered, "in the middle of the street with six guns on us? With the women standing there? You're too damned hot-headed, Eric, anyone ever point that out to you?"

"At least we wouldn't be locked up in here waiting to find out what those wolves have in mind."

"We're better off in here, Eric," Ki reasoned. "Cadge is right about one thing—a gun battle in the middle of the street in broad daylight wasn't the way to go."

"At least I had my gun! What the hell *can* we do in here?" Eric demanded.

"That remains to be seen," Ki answered quietly.

"We better goddamn well figure out something and soon," Eric said, still simmering. "When those outlaws get drunked up good and proper they'll be back—and they'll take the women first, you can bet on that."

Eric continued to rant and grumble. None of it was very helpful. Jessica found her way to where Ki was perched on a broken crate and asked, "Well, what do you think?"

"Several advantages for us, one big one for them."

"Their guns."

Ki nodded in the darkness. "We know that they're drinking, and that will slow them down. And they don't know anything about us at all."

Cadge was listening in. "What do you mean, Ki? They don't know that you do all that kicking and fancy stuff?"

"That," Ki answered, "and they do not know that Jessica is capable of a little 'fancy stuff.' Nor do they know that you are a former professional boxer, Cadge. I think they've singled out Eric as the one to watch. The rest of us seemed to be perceived as beneath considering. They won't expect any trouble at all from us."

"I'm not sure," Cadge pointed out, "that all of our little advantages outweigh their one big one."

Neither was Ki, but he hoped it was enough. The main thing, he believed, was to surprise the outlaws, to attack, and to attack with force.

"When they do come," Ki pointed out, "it is very unlikely that six of them will come together. Two men, perhaps three with arms, but off-guard. They can't come through the door more than one at a time. That's when we have to make our move, as swiftly and silently as possible."

"Sure." Eric grew enthusiastic. "Then out the back-alley door and away, right?"

"No," Ki said. "I'm afraid not. They all have to be taken care of. How else are we going to retrieve the fuel oil?"

A brief silence followed that. Ki was right—they were going to have to eliminate the entire gang in one way or another before they could make an escape.

"You've got some kind of plan, don't you, Ki?" Cadge Dana asked a little nervously.

"Just what I've already told you."

"You told us the *what,*" Eric growled, "you ain't told us the *how.*"

"We can't plan much," Ki said. "We'll have to take what is offered."

"And in the meantime we just sit and wait?" Eric asked.

"And in the meantime, we sit. And wait."

There wasn't much conversation after that. The rats scuttling across the floor, nesting in the rags and old lumber, made more noise than the hostages did.

Ki had dozed off when, hours later Cadge nudged him roughly with an elbow.

101

"What is it?"

"Listen," Dana whispered. "They're coming."

Ki was instantly alert. Moving to the door he put his ear next to it. Cadge was right. Two men—or three—scuffling along in high-heeled boots. One of them laughed and the other one joined in. Two of them—unless the third had a different sort of sense of humor.

Ki stepped to the side of the door as the bar was lifted and flipped aside. When the door opened the light from without showed Melinda and Sperry back against one wall, Eric truculently sat in the center of the room, Jessica on her feet to one side, Dana sitting on a crate.

"Judge decided . . ." the man with the patch said with a dirty laugh, "jury gets to take the prisoners home. It'll be ladies first, of course."

He had his rifle barrel in front of him as he spoke. Ki wasn't going to wait for a better opportunity. One might not come. The *te* master's hand shot out and gripped the barrel of the Winchester, ripping it from Riz's hand. Yanking the outlaw into the room, Ki spun, his knee taking the outlaw in the groin, doubling him up. Dana finished him with a right hook.

It was so fast that the man in the hallway, half drunk, didn't have time to yell out or cock his rifle. He never got the time.

Ki had already planned his movement, and as the outlaw backed away, Ki's spinning kick slammed into the outlaw's throat, banging him back against the wall. Ki took the rifle from his hands as he fell, to keep it from clattering against the floor.

Grabbing the man's boots, Ki dragged him into the storage room, where he joined his companion on the floor.

Ki spoke quickly. "Melinda, Professor, Jessica, Eric—out the back door quickly. Find a place to hide and wait—"

"No," Jessica said, slipping a revolver from Riz's holster. "You think I'm missing out on this, you're crazy."

Ki didn't argue with the lady—he seldom had any success doing that. Eric was insistent too. "I owe 'em. I'm fighting."

Ki didn't debate with Eric either. "Professor?"

"I'm going. I'm not a warrior. Nor is Melinda."

102

Melinda started to speak, to reach for Ki's hand, but he was distracted and her father was already tugging her away toward the alley door.

"Armed?" Ki asked Cadge. The former boxer held up his rifle. "All right—they're better armed. We have surprise, let's use it. We have no way of knowing if they're all in the lobby, upstairs, or split up, maybe some outside the hotel. Be careful. Jessica—"

"I said I was going, Ki."

Ki just turned and started up the hallway, his throwing stars in hand. He put out each lantern as he passed it. There was no sense backlighting themselves.

Four against four, Ki was thinking. And they were half-drunk. The difference was that those four were cold-blooded killers. When it came time to shoot they would shoot to kill without hesitation. Dana and Eric were fighters, but hardly professionals at it.

The other difference was that Jessica was with them. It took only one bullet to ruin the attack and a good part of Ki's life—one bullet tagging Jessica Starbuck. It had to be done quickly, without a single slip-up.

At the end of the corridor Ki could see the broken-down settee and the crossed legs of a man sitting on it. Behind him Jessica muffled the action of her revolver with her left hand and cocked the borrowed Colt.

Looking back, Ki nodded. It was do it now or do it never.

He stepped into the room.

Jessica saw Ki send a throwing star into the throat of a seated man and then dive for cover as a Colt sprayed bullets in his direction. Jessie was ready, and using both hands she squeezed off three shots. The first one would have been enough to take out the outlaw. It went in his right eye and exploded out the back of his skull.

"Look out!" Dana shouted.

At the head of the staircase a shirtless Lavender had appeared, pistol in each hand. Cadge's Winchester spat lead at the outlaw king and he toppled forward, rattling down the steps.

Bullets thudded into the wall beside Cadge's head. The

cross-eyed bandit with the blond hair had been posted outside. Hearing the shots, he had burst into the room to open up with his twin Colts. Cadge hit the floor, taking Jessica with him.

Eric remained erect. He took careful aim and fired. A spinning .44-40 slug found the soft belly of the outlaw and jackknifed him. His pistol exploded twice more, sending lead into the ceiling over him, and then he pitched forward to lie in a pool of his own blood.

"Anybody counting?" Cadge asked from the floor.

"That's four," Ki answered quietly.

Slowly Cadge rose. Jessica gave him a brief fiery look. "Dammit, I had him in my sights!" Then she sighed, holstered the pistol, and smiled.

"I think I'm hit," Eric said very quietly. Then his legs buckled. Ki caught him before he hit the floor, and placed him in an overstuffed chair. "I think he got me good," the mechanic said. When he pulled his hand away from his chest they could see that his assessment was too accurate.

"We can get that bullet out," Cadge Dana said.

"Yeah? Show me your medical diploma." He sat erect suddenly and blinked away the pain. "Yeah . . . tell the professor to back those needle screws off a quarter of an inch or so . . . you know . . ."

And that was it. Eric's chin fell forward, struck his chest, and he was gone. Ki wiped a hand across his mouth. The operation was a failure. Any military operation is a failure if you lose one man.

"Bury him?" Cadge asked, looking around the room. "The others?"

"Leave them," Ki answered.

"What about the two in the storeroom?"

"Let them figure it out," Ki said without sympathy. "Let's find our bedrolls—the professor's gold—Jessica's gun—and get the hell out of this miserable hole."

"He went out like a man," Cadge said of Eric. "I just never could figure out what was going on inside of him."

"I don't think he knew, himself," Jessica said. "Come on, let's get moving."

They rigged up a crude travois, and, using the outlaws' horses, they started back along the road toward the balloon.

The professor and Melinda held back at first and then came forward out of the trees. "When we heard the horses, we thought it was them."

"No," Ki said, "they won't be coming."

"Eric?"

"He won't be coming either. Sorry."

The professor said, "But Eric was going to reset the burner."

"He said to back the needle screws off a quarter of an inch or so. If you know what he meant."

"Yes, yes, of course. Sorry about Eric. He was a strange man but I'll miss him."

"Let's get that old drum off and get this one in place, Cadge, if you're able."

"I'll try."

"If the women will take the rest of our gear on board?"

"Sure," Jessie agreed. "Melissa?"

It didn't take long to unstrap the old barrel and overboard it. Getting the new, full one up was more of a battle, but Ki rigged a pulley, and, using a horse, they got it on deck and in place before the professor was ready to run the line to his adjusted burner.

Cadge and Jessica scrambled up to the roof of the cabin. The wind was worse. It nearly knocked Jessica Starbuck off the cabin. Cadge crouched beside the distracted professor and pointed at the burner.

"Will it work?"

Sperry shrugged. "We'll know when we light it. Fuel in place, is it?"

At Cadge's nod, Sperry primed the burner. The second match brought the burner to life with a sputter and the familiar pop. Then it went out. Sperry got back to it with his screwdriver.

The next try was as much a failure, and there were concerned glances all around. Maybe they would miss Eric even more than they had imagined.

The third try lit cleanly and the flame in the burner built to its normal height. Grinning weakly, the professor stood and told them so. "Got it—I think."

It was an hour before the crimson balloon was fully inflated. They cast off the lines and lifted into the gray, windy skies, leaving Silver Springs behind.

They ran the burner full-open as they crept higher into the pine-clad mountains. The heads of the Rocky Mountains were ominously far above them.

"Weather's getting worse," Jessica said. "There's ice on a couple of gondola cables."

"We can't set down again this afternoon," Ki said, shouting above the whistling wind. "We'll have to get over the summit now."

"Over those?" Jessica said dubiously, looking at the four-teen-thousand-foot-high pyramidal mountain to the north.

"There's a pass. Melinda said it was called Last Stretch Pass. Supposed to be dead ahead somewhere."

All Jessica could see dead ahead was a wall of mountains. It wasn't really reassuring to watch the balloon drift straight at the face of the mountains.

"We had luck last time we tried this trick," Jessie said. "A lot of luck. Think we can repeat?"

Ki didn't answer. What was there to say? He wiped a hand across his face. There was frost in his eyebrows now, and the light rain was turning to sleet.

Cadge Dana, wearing a lifeline again, crept toward them across the icy deck, bundled in a sweater, coat, scarf, and leather cap. "When it rains, it pours," was the first thing he said.

"What?"

"Look behind us," Cadge said.

Slowly they turned and stared in disbelief. Through the mist and sleet the great black-and-white-striped balloon rose steadily toward them.

"Tyler Gregor's back. I guess you didn't get that burner after all, Ki."

"You'd better break out the weapons," Ki said decisively. "Try to keep the actions warm somehow."

"You don't think they'd start shooting here! Now? Haven't they got their hands full trying to get over the mountains?"

"I think," Ki answered, "they will start shooting as soon as they get in range. These men are cold-blooded killers. This is a good place to put us down, wouldn't you say? Who would ever find us? We'd just be listed as lost in the newspapers."

"Like McCarthy's rig and Chambers' crew are lost. I'll get the guns," Cadge said. "I mean to live long enough to write this story."

The striped balloon closed on them as they rose higher. Everyone had trouble breathing at the higher elevation. There was no way at all to stay warm. Melinda and her father crouched near the burner, but it was obviously doing them no good either. The burner was wide open, trying to counteract the effects of the cold.

"Where is that damned pass?" Cadge asked through chattering teeth. "I can't see anything at all."

"I can't either. We can't do a thing but hold on and hope Melinda's charts are correct."

"And that a gust of wind doesn't whip us against one of those peaks. Christ, look at that ridge! Like sawteeth."

The mist and sleet had stopped, but they were so near to the mountains now that they were showered with snow lifted from the peaks by the relentless wind. The black-and-white balloon grew steadily nearer, like a shadow cast against the sky by their own craft.

Ice clung to the gondola, varnishing the steel cables, forming icicles along the rail. They were kept busy knocking it off with hammers. The extra weight of the ice could drag the balloon down if left unchecked.

There was still no sign of the pass, and the rifles on the gondola of the black-and-white balloon opened up again, although the sniping was sporadic. Ki felt a bullet strike a cable inches above his hand, and he wondered what would happen if one of those was severed.

He fired back a pair of shots. Probably useless. He aimed at the head of the balloon until Melinda pointed out, "You could puncture a hundred bullet-sized holes in that, Ki, and it wouldn't go down"

Ahead the sky was dismally dark. The wind shook the gondoia violently and lightning flashed against the sky, followed by close thunder.

"Terrific," Ki muttered. He decided then and there that

whatever project Jessica Starbuck took up next, it had better be on the ground. Jessica was thinking much the same thing when a gust of wind lifted the gondola nearly sideways. She fell hard, ripping the knees out of her jeans as she groped for a handhold.

"There it is!" Melinda shouted excitedly. "The pass—do you see it, Ki?"

Ki didn't, as the clouds shut off all view ahead, but they parted again, briefly, and in that moment Ki did see the pass. Nearly U-shaped, it was miles wide and seemed to offer a safe passage through the mountains.

The storm grew in intensity. There was neither rain nor snow, but the electrical display was amazing. Forked lightning struck out in all directions, and once a bridge of bone-white light arced across the storm-darkened sky, producing intense close thunder that rattled their eardrums and left them temporarily deaf.

The gap was gone again, vanished behind the wall of black clouds. There was nothing to do but sail straight ahead on the whims of the wind and hope for the best.

Behind them the Gregor balloon, if it was still in the air, was equally invisible.

"Maybe the bastard rammed a peak," Cadge muttered.

Jessica clutched his arm. "The gap, Cadge. Look!"

There it was, suddenly, a haven from the crazed winds. The pass opened up before them and they were into it, flying at a safe altitude, the force of the wind lessened by sheltering walls of stone.

Their speed increased and they sailed over a desolate landscape of dark rock and stone. Beyond the pass they could lose altitude safely, eliminating ice, with luck dodging the storm.

Ahead, only briefly, Ki thought he saw a long grassy plain far below, stretching out for miles. He saw that, and then Melinda shrieked and he spun. She was frozen in place, pointing up. Gregor was directly above them, dropping toward their balloon like a stone.

The gun bellowed smoke and fire, and this time, instead of using a rifle, they had gone for a double-barreled shotgun. A hole the size of both of Ki's hands appeared in the red silk of the balloon. He ducked, sent a *shuriken* whizzing toward the gunner's head and missed as the wind bent the trajectory of his throw.

Cadge Dana opened up with a Winchester, sending a dozen rounds upward, trying to drive the attackers off. Brass casings littered the deck of the gondola, but the shotgun fired again, and a second hole appeared in the silk.

Jessica Starbuck knelt at the rail, emptying her pistol at the gondola above them. The shotgunner fell back from the rail and the balloon veered away.

Ki looked upward at the balloon fabric and then shouted to Melinda, "What's that going to do?"

"Take us down," was her answer. "It's going to take us down."

Chapter 11

They sailed on through the pass, although it was obvious they were losing altitude. Still, they had several hundred feet of clearance, and if they went down, at least it wouldn't be in the high reaches of the Rockies.

Above them the sky clattered with thunder and lightning. Gregor, apparently trying to make another pass at them, had lifted and then begun a descent. They were all watching, ready for more shooting, as the lightning struck. A flash of light and then Gregor's balloon was hit. It began a slow, crazy spiraling, as smoke trailed from the fabric of his black-and-white balloon. He had been above them, but in less than a minute he was below them, his gondola only a few feet from the ground as the crew tried to do something to slow the descent.

Then Gregor's craft was lost again in the clouds. Simultaneously the land fell away beneath Sperry's balloon and they began a rapid descent toward the long, grassy plain Ki had seen.

"Will we make it?" Jessica looked at the punctured balloon, which was obviously deflating no matter what Sperry and his burner could do. Fabric fluttered in the wind and they were dropping rapidly.

Green flatland spun up toward them as they slid past mountain peaks, jagged ridges, timbered mountain meadows. There was nothing to do but hold on, and Ki knew it. Still he kept his eyes riveted to the torn balloon, watching the rips grow larger with each moment, as if that were helping a thing.

Their descent seemed to slow as they got lower and the air

warmer, but it was going to be a rough landing nevertheless. When they hit, it was jarring. The gondola upended and Cadge went flying. Ki was thrown from one end of the deck to the other, rolling along it like a billiard ball. The wind tugged them along for half a mile before the lift was gone completely from the balloon and they sat motionless in the center of a seemingly endless green prairie, the crimson balloon slowly deflating as the burner huffed away uselessly.

In a minute even that sound was gone as Sperry switched off. Then there was nothing but the fabric ripping in the wind, and the whistle of the wind itself racing across the long plain.

It took Cadge ten minutes to catch up. He was holding his side and gimping along on a bad leg, but he was alive. Jessica leaped from the ravaged gondola and rushed to him, holding him to her as the cold wind lifted her long, honey-blond hair.

"Lifeline did a hell of a lot of good," Cadge complained, showing her the end of the tether, which had snapped.

"It could have happened at eight thousand feet," Jessica Starbuck pointed out.

Cadge rubbed his head. "Feels like it did."

Beside the gondola Melinda looked up at the rapidly flattening balloon, its fabric torn to shreds. "Looks like your toy's broken, Daddy," she said to her father, who appeared to be in mild shock.

"Over. They did it finally. It's over."

"Don't tell me you're going to give up," Ki said warmly. "Not you—after all this, Professor."

"What else can I do?" he asked, shrugging his narrow shoulders.

"Can we patch it?" Ki asked.

"Not here, not without new material. Did you see the lower tear? It must be five feet long."

"Then," Ki said, looking across the plain, "we need some help."

"Help?" the professor said. "We need a miracle."

"There's nothing to do but walk away from it, Ki," Melinda said.

"We're going to have to walk, that's for sure. Do your charts show a town around anywhere?"

111

"I didn't look. I don't know."

"Get them and look."

Jessica asked, "What are you thinking, Ki?"

"Just what I said—we have to walk out anyway. Let's take the balloon with us."

Jessica just looked at him. "Do you know what that thing weighs?"

"We'll have to leave the gondola and fashion another one."

The professor didn't have any optimism left. "Ki, that gondola was specially built of rattan to my specifications. It took two months to build."

"Yes, but we don't need it. Look, we've come this far—think of what we've been through. The rest of the trip may be longer, but with the mountains, the desert, and Gregor behind us we can float to St. Louis easily. Any handyman can slap something together that we can use as a gondola. Smaller, maybe, maybe crude, but it can be done. All we need is the burner and the balloon itself. Or isn't it worth it to you anymore?"

"Of course it's worth it. But Ki, the fabric alone weighs more than you could imagine."

"And there are five of us to carry it," Ki pointed out. "I'm not ready to give up, and I don't think you are. Nor is Jessica, nor your daughter. Not now. We've endured to much already."

"You're right." Sperry fingered his brow. "It's just that I'm exhausted, that this last episode, to be honest, has taken the fight out of me. Of course you're right, Ki," he said brightening. "Of course we will go on! And when I do fly to the moon—"

"You'll do it alone," Ki said. "I assure you."

"What do we do, Ki?" Jessica asked. She was sitting on the cold earth, examining a torn knee.

He looked up. "Wait for that thing to deflate and then fold it as tightly as we can."

"Then we walk."

"Then," he answered, "we walk."

"I don't know exactly where we are, Ki. Maybe Melinda can find a nearby town, but I doubt it. I do know one thing—we're in Indian country again, and I'm not talking about a few wandering desert hunters."

112

"I know," Ki said in a quieter voice. "Utes, perhaps Jicarilla Apache, if they haven't started toward their winter *rancherias* in Mexico."

"Early for that, Ki," Jessica said as she stretched out a hand and Ki tugged her to her feet.

"Yes, it is, isn't it?"

"You think it's a good idea to encourage the professor?"

"Do you want to tell him, Jessica? Tell him that we're in the worst position we've been in since we left San Francisco, that the odds of flying on to St. Louis are roughly as good as those of our staying alive? Roughly nil?"

Jessica couldn't answer. She shook her head, set her hat on her head, and walked toward the balloon. There was a lot of work to be done if they were going to fold that massive globe and, along with the burner and necessary cables, trek out to something that might resemble civilization.

There was nothing to do but get started.

It wasn't until nightfall that they had things bundled up. The silk was rolled into a long, tight tube which took two, preferably three people to lug. On this night they let it lie against the dew-soaked earth, ate cold food from cold tins, and tried to sleep with the cold wind blowing.

In the morning they rose, and with Ki packing the burner on his back, with the women and Cadge sharing the burden of the collapsed and folded balloon, they started walking the long plains toward a distant flyspeck on the map Melinda had located.

It was exhausting. No one had much breath for conversation at that point. Dana was especially silent. Jessica asked him, "What are you doing, writing this up in your head?"

"Writing it up?" Dana panted. "I'm only thinking about how we're going to survive it."

Melinda, now carrying only the all-important mail sack, staggered, and Ki reached out to help her.

"You all right?"

"Sure, nothing like a walk in the fresh air," she answered. "Ki, you do know we have company, don't you?"

"I saw them half a mile back. Are they still there?"

"Yes. Eight or ten of them, I think, all mounted. Are they what I think they are?"

113

"Yes. Apaches," Ki answered.

Cadge said only "it figures" as he shifted his share of the balloon onto his other shoulder.

"Shouldn't we do something?" Professor Sperry asked.

"What? Attack? Run? Hide? Sorry, professor, I don't believe there's a thing we can do."

"Why are they just watching us?"

"There could be a number of reasons. Probably we're the strangest collection of travelers they've ever seen. Must wonder what we could possibly be up to."

"Do you think they saw us come down?"

"No telling. Probably they see everything that goes on in this country."

"Ki," Jessica asked, "what are the other reasons—besides curiosity?"

"They could be waiting for a leader to arrive, or the rest of their warriors. Maybe there's an army patrol somewhere around, though that seems unlikely."

"Or . . . ?" Cadge prompted.

"Or they're just waiting until we drop and they can move in and take what they want."

"How far do we have to go yet, Melinda?" Cadge asked.

"Not far."

"How far is that?"

Reluctantly she answered, "Maybe fifty miles. There's a place up along the Canadian River called Desperation."

"The town would have a name like that," Cadge Dana muttered. He looked to the north and saw the Indians himself, briefly. They were riding parallel to their party, at times visible, at times lost behind the low, rolling hills.

By sundown they were walking with wooden legs, backs and shoulders aching and knotted. They were thirsty, hungry, and exhausted. The professor had had the lightest burden to carry, but he was worst off.

They stopped at a small creek which wound off the prairie, flowed through a small stand of cottonwood trees and bloomless wild roses, and then lost itself again on the prairie.

"Well," Cadge said irritably, "we can't walk all night." He had reason to be irritable and they all knew it. His would

114

continued to leak blood. He belonged in bed and not trekking across the prairie.

"Let's put it down," Ki agreed, and they let the huge roll of silk drop to the ground. The burner and mailbag followed, and they stood there looking at each other.

Sperry put it into words: "Will the Apaches be coming now?"

"I don't know. Their behavior has been a little peculiar." Ki looked toward the dying sun moving downward toward the cradle of the mountains, reddening the empty sky. "If they mean to attack at all . . . I think it would be soon."

"Ki," Jessica said, "the creek."

"What about it?"

"It would be faster than walking."

Melinda asked, "What are you talking about?"

"It's deep enough, wide enough. It's flowing southeast. It should only get wider. If it rains upcountry as it has been, the current will increase. I'm talking, Melinda, about rafting downriver."

"But we don't even know which creek this is, where it goes," the redhead objected.

"You have your charts. We know one thing. It goes in the direction we want to go."

"And away from the Apaches," Cadge said. "Do you think they'd give us time to do what you're planning?"

"You'll have to ask them," Jessica said. "All I know is that we're not going to walk out of here the way we're going."

"We have no way to build a raft," Sperry pointed out. Jessica didn't agree.

"There's always a way. Dead branches, lashed with lines from the balloon. It'll have to be a large raft, but it doesn't have to be pretty. It just has to float!"

"In the morning—" Cadge began.

"We can begin right now," Jessica said, the idea catching fire in her mind. "We have to."

"But it's nearly dark."

"We have time to scour these cottonwoods for anything usable. Drag the wood into camp. We can lash it together by firelight."

115

"Start a fire? Tonight, with the Apaches out there?" Dana said in disbelief.

"Why not?" Jessica asked. "They know exactly where we are anyway. I don't know what kind of chance we have, Cadge, but the sooner we try it the better that chance is."

Dana didn't like it. Melinda didn't like it. Hell, Jessica didn't like it, but no one could come up with an alternative— except to wait until the Apaches made up their minds what they were going to do, and that didn't seem like much of an alternative.

They got to work by the light of the setting sun. Tired as they were, they moved with the energy of desperation. Melinda checked her charts and was uncertain. As Ki came in, towing two large crooked cottonwood logs behind him, she said, "I can't tell where the creek flows. There's a dotted 'guess line' on the map. This is still pretty much unexplored territory, Ki. It may flow into the Canadian or even the Cimarron, which would do just as well for us . . . or it may go nowhere at all and leave us worse off than before."

"It flows into the Canadian," Ki said firmly.

"But you can't know that!"

"No." Ki smiled and kissed the woman. "But I refuse to grow negative about it now. We've decided. Let's do it!"

"And if Father ask me?" Melinda asked.

"Tell him—it flows into the Canadian. Ki said so."

Ki said so, but Ki had no idea in the world where the creek flowed. No matter. It had to be done. They weren't going to walk out, and if the Apaches took the notion, they were going to overrun the camp and finish the journey in a spectacular and bloody way. Jessica was right—this chance, feeble as it was, was their only chance.

Feverishly Ki began lashing their odd collection of logs together into a jerry-built raft. It bulged and bent, but it would float. The cottonwood logs were long dead, dry, and light. The professor was visibly distressed as Ki and Dana cut lines from his precious balloon, but these could be repaired or replaced, Ki pointed out. There was no replacing their blood if the Apaches hit them.

"Creek's running faster," Jessica pointed out. "It's still raining in the mountians."

116

Ki glanced at the dark creek. Jessica was right. The water had risen and was definitely moving faster. Now if they could finish their work and get the raft in the river before the Indians came . . . if the damned thing floated well enough to support their weight and the weight of the balloon. . . . If.

They dragged the raft to the creek. Dana held on to a mooring line while the others dragged the balloon onto the raft. Good enough so far—the raft didn't sink perceptibly. It was a huge, ragged thing, ten by fifteen feet. Still, Melinda was dubious. It had to carry the additional weight of five adults.

The burner was carried on board, and the mail sack. Melinda and the professor boarded carefully, trying to balance their weight. Ki and Dana, who had lashed the line to the nearest tree, were next. Jessica, carrying her bedroll, trotted toward the raft. The sun was gone. Their fire burned dully.

It was then that the Apaches attacked.

Dana shouted and fired at a dimly seen target in the woods, his rifle spewing flame. Jessica dropped the bedroll and unholstered her .38 revolver.

She dove to the ground as an arrow whipped past her head and embedded itself in a twisted cottonwood. Jessie saw an Indian in front of her and took a badly aimed shot at him. Racing toward the creek she drew her pocketknife and cut the line, and the raft started drifting downstream.

Ki leaped to his feet, filling his hand with his *shurikens*. The Apache arrow hummed unseen through the darkness and took Ki in the shoulder. He staggered back, fell over the balloon, and was dragged to the far side of the roll of fabric.

"Jessica . . ." Ki said, and he struggled to get to his feet. It was obvious he wasn't going to make it. They simply held him down as gunshots and arrows filled the night and the raft floated away on the dark creek.

Jessica started to leap for the raft but jumped back again as an Apache from the trees to the north bore down on her, his rifle flashing twice in the night, the bullets tearing the bark from the tree beside her.

Dropping to one knee, Jessica got off two shots, the second stopping the onrushing Apache in his tracks. To her left more Indians appeared, and Jessica took to her heels.

117

Weaving through the trees she heard the bullets whipping past her in the darkness. The raft was in sight, but it was being carried along rapidly by the current. She just wasn't going to catch up.

She heard a shout ahead of her and went to the ground, crawling into a tangle of wild roses and blackthorn. The two Indians emerged slowly from the darkness and moved toward her, cutting sharp silhouettes against the starry sky.

Jessie slowly, silently cocked her double-action revolver and sighted on the lead warrior.

Her front sight tracked the man as he walked carefully forward, his moccasined feet making not a whisper of sound. By the way the Apaches were searching she knew that they realized she had been left behind. Instead of pursuing the raft on horseback they had determined to search for the one who had been left behind.

The man crept past her. She could have spit and hit him. He crouched, and with infinite patience waited, listening to the sounds of the night, the loudest of which was the rushing river.

Jessica saw him gesture to the second man and then move on. She slowly let out her breath and shifted her sights to the second Apache.

Now what? Wait until they had had the time to comb every inch of the woods? They were in no hurry. They had all night to try to find the white woman, all night to do whatever in hell they had in mind.

Ki. Ki was hurt, and Jessica knew it. She had seen him fall. How bad was it? She had to catch up with the others; to remain here was to die.

Muted voices from the north drifted on the wind. The man positioned just before her had crouched, watching, Winchester repeater across his knees.

A shot from the .38 would eliminate him, but it would bring the others on the run. It would have to be done silently, if possible, the way Ki would do it. But Jessica, scrapper that she was, was not Ki, the *te* master.

There wasn't much choice. The others would be back soon as they swept the woods looking for the lone white woman.

Jessica drew her legs up under her, planting her feet. If she

118

could get behind the Apache somehow . . . Her plans suddenly exploded in her face.

The Indian was a hunter and a warrior, and some small noise brought him to his feet, brought his head around so that his eyes locked with those of Jessica Starbuck. Grinning, he leaped toward her, and the .38 Colt did its work, a bullet tagging the brave's heart, its thunder rattling through the trees.

There were shouts behind her and the sounds of rushing feet. There was only one way to go, and Jessie took it. The creek was cold and dark and rapid, but she plunged into its current, letting it spin her away down a dark corridor as the Apaches on shore emptied their rifles into the water.

Chapter 12

The current was swift and swirling, the water icy and black. Jessica was carried away through the night, her head bobbing above the surface. Gradually the Apache rifles fell silent, but she felt no safer. An hour or two in the water and she would be dead—but to try to swim to shore and outrun the mounted Indians was even more dangerous.

Her only hope was catching up with the raft somehow, but that too seemed unlikely. For now she could only float along, trying to keep her head above water, enduring the numbing cold . . . hoping that the Apaches couldn't catch up.

"Put in to shore!" Cadge Dana said violently. "Dammit, Jessica's back there."

Melinda was crouched over Ki, trying to help him. In the darkness she couldn't see much but the shaft of the Apache arrow protruding from his shoulder. Ki was perfectly still, silent. He was obviously in pain, but he refused to acknowledge it.

"We can't stop," Sperry said. "Not with the Indians out there. They're sure to catch up." He held on as the raft dipped through a trough in the creek. "We have to keep going."

"For the sake of the damned race?"

"For Ki's sake," Sperry said quietly. "For my daughter's."

"If you can't wait, put into shore. I'm getting off and I'm going back," Dana insisted.

"What are you going to do, one man alone?"

"What I'm not going to do, Professor Sperry, is leave her back there by herself."

"Father," Melinda said, "we have to wait for Jessica. No matter what."

"But—"

"We have to wait. We can put it to a vote if you like. You know what Cadge's vote is, what Ki's would be. I agree. We have to wait and see if Jessica hasn't escaped. You would never forgive yourself otherwise, and you know it."

"Yes, yes," Sperry said, wiping back his thin white hair. "You're right, of course. Sorry, Dana. To tell you the truth I think I was scared out of my mind. I haven't been thinking about anything but escape."

"All right. Forget the explanations. We're all scared. See if we can find a place to tie up. The more hidden the better. But let's not wait too long. Every minute we travel downstream lessens Jessica's chances of survival. There! See that oxbow with the big elms? Can we make it into that?"

"We can try."

Using the crude paddles they had fashioned, poling along the bottom when the water got shallow enough, they moved into an oxbow off the main river. Great willows arched over the stream, and a thick stand of elms screened out the sky. The moon was rising somewhere out of their sight; the sky was paling slightly, the river taking on a dull sheen.

"She'll never find us here," Melinda said worriedly.

"Then," Cadge swore, "by God, I'll find her. If necessary, come morning, I'll start back upriver alone." Ki muttered something that might have been an objection. It was hard to tell. He had been hit hard and was a little out of his head. Cadge turned, crouched, and smiled. "If you're arguing with me, Ki, you know you're wasting your time—and you know damned well that you'd do exactly the same thing, no matter if it cost you your neck."

Dana splashed ashore and tied up the raft. Leaving the professor to his worries, and Melinda to tend to Ki, he crossed the narrow crescent of land separating the oxbow from the river proper and sat down, waiting, his eyes searching the night.

"Make it, Jessica. Be all right," he whispered to the night sky.

121

It was no good, she realized. Jessica had been in the water for half an hour and her legs and arms were numb, her lungs fiery. She thought once that the cold water was going to stop her heart. It started thumping away crazily, protesting the temperature and exertion.

She had to get out of the river. The Apaches suddenly seemed a preferable alternative to the cold. She stroked toward the far bank and crawled up onto the shore beneath the willows that stood there. The stars glared down; the moon was slowly rising. Jessica Starbuck, shivering violently, stripped off her clothing, belted her handgun on around her naked waist, and started south, jogging through the trees.

Rocks and tree roots tore at her feet. She kept running, not so much to leave the Indians behind but simply to stay warm. It was crazy! Running naked through the night trying to catch the raft, which was probably long gone—which *was* long gone if one of the men, or Melinda, hadn't been overwhelmed by some chivalrous notion.

She held her breasts to keep them from swinging so hard, wishing for one of the few times in her life that she hadn't been so well-endowed by nature.

The Apache was suddenly there, sitting his paint pony. He was no wooden-faced Apache, fearing to show emotion. He was grinning from ear to ear, and why not? Out of the night woods, a beautiful bare-assed naked white woman had come rushing toward him.

Jessica drew her revolver and fired, but nothing happened. The soaking in the river had finished her ammunition. She came to a halt, slowly holstered her useless weapon, and started veering away from the trail at a casual walk.

The Apache turned his horse's head and followed.

"Give me another few yards and I'm gone," Jessica muttered. Back into the river. It was the only chance she had.

The Apache wasn't about to let a prize like this one go so easily. Jessica, walking faster now, looked back to watch the man dismount, drop the reins to his pony, and suddenly dash after her.

Jessie reacted, breaking into a run as she wove through the

trees, her hair streaming out behind her, her eyes on the dark creek ahead. She felt a hand on her shoulder, and then the weight of the man on her back, and she fell, scratching and clawing, twisting around to fight back.

The Apache had caught her, but it was like catching a bobcat bare-handed. Forked, stiffened fingers were driven into the Indian's eyes and he howled with pain, covering his face as Jessica drove her knee up into his groin.

She rolled away from underneath him and stood panting, facing him. The Apache, the grin gone now, his eyes bloody, leaped for her. He caught a side-kick to the face for his trouble. Deciding enough was enough, he drew his rawhide-handled knife.

Holding it low he moved in on Jessica, who backed away until her butt was pressed against a willow tree.

"Now, woman," the Apache said, laughing. Whether he was trying to scare her or meant to knife her, the blade slashed close to Jessie's belly. She caught the wrist, turned and hip-rolled the astonished Indian to the ground.

He rose quickly, angrily. His knife, unfortunately for him, was now in the hellcat white woman's hand. He could have turned and gone then, but his manhood wouldn't allow it. He dove at Jessica and she slashed upward with the knife, ripping through his abdomen, the point of the knife touching heart muscle, rupturing it. The Apache fell back, clutching his gut, staring in shocked disbelief at the woman.

Was she a woman, or some spirit-thing? How had such a small, naked woman overpowered him? In a moment he was past considering it. He took two staggering steps backward and then fell to the ground, dead.

Jessica stood there a minute, teeth chattering with the cold, heart racing with the savagery of the moment. Then she started back toward the trail and the Apache's abandoned pony.

Cadge Dana cocked his head, his body coming erect. He could hear someone coming, a horse pounding up the trail beside the creek. He reached for his Winchester and levered in a round.

The Indian pony was in sight now and Dana took a test-sighting on the dark figure behind the trees. Any closer . . . The Indian had long trailing hair—light-colored hair—and Cadge lowered the rifle.

"Jessica!" He yelled again, louder, and the horse drew up. She started the pony across the creek and Cadge saw she wore only a blanket across her shoulders. She was dirty-faced, her hair tangled. But she was alive.

Jessica slipped from the horse and rushed to Cadge. He held her, petting her hair. "What happened? What in the hell happened to you, Jessie?"

"Later. You have the raft still? Let's get it back in the water and get the hell out of here."

"Yeah," Cadge agreed. "Let's get out of here."

"Ki? Is Ki hurt? I thought I saw him go down," Jessica said as they hurried back to the raft.

"He took an arrow in the shoulder."

"Serious?"

"It's hard to see much or do anything until dawn. Melinda's been trying."

Sperry, a gun in his hands for the first time since the crazy journey had begun, gawked at the sight of the half-naked Jessica Starbuck.

"Made it . . . You made it," Sperry said.

"Where's Ki?"

"Right there. Cast off, Cadge."

Cadge had already cut the line, and was now poling them out into the current, which carried them off down the swollen creek as the moon hovered above the trees on the shoreline.

Jessica crouched over Ki, touched his hot forehead, and looked at the arrow, trying to guess at the extent of the damage.

"Here," Melinda said, handing Jessie a pair of her spare jeans and a blouse. Gratefully, Jessica dressed in warm clothing again and returned to watching Ki, sitting beside him, holding his hand as the raft sailed on.

Sunrise found them well down the river. They were no longer concerned about the Apaches following them, but only about Ki, who was obviously badly injured. The arrow had to come out, and now.

"Put in to shore," Jessica told Cadge. "We can't do it on a rocking raft."

"All right. Who's the surgeon, me?"

"Have you dealt with arrows before?" At Cadge's negative shake of the head, Jessica said, "It's me, then. I've dug out a few."

Ashore, they carried Ki to a flat clearing, laid him on a blanket, and started a small fire to sterilize the knife. Ki was in a sweat, his eyes bright, but he knew what was happening. Melinda used the fire to brew some tea; Ki would need something hot. Besides, it kept her mind off what Jessica was going to do.

"You can't shove it on through?" Cadge asked, meaning the arrow shaft. He had always heard that was the way to do it. Shove it on through, no matter what pain it cost the patient, snap off the arrow head, and yank it back out.

"It's up against bone," Jessie said. "Besides, I've seen that technique kill men. Pushing it on through might sever the artery an arrow's just missed, or clip the nerves a man needs to make his body work. I'll have to cut it out. Right, Ki?"

Ki's answer was a distant smile. He knew well enough what was going on, but he didn't have the strength just then to answer.

The knife bit deep. Jessica had to try thinking of Ki as a stranger or a hunk of beef. He didn't feel it as she dug around for the arrowhead. At the first cut he had gone out—even Ki could only take so much.

Melinda wiped away the blood as Jessica worked. After a second deep incision Jessica braced herself and tugged. The bloody obsidian arrowhead came free, and they got to work patching up the wound as best they could.

Back on the river, they sailed on, still not knowing exactly where the creek terminated. Sperry sat brooding. From time to time he would look up and say, "I've caused a lot of trouble. Pain. Death."

"We'll make it," Jessie said soothingly.

"If we find a town—I'm ready to quit. It's not worth it." Sperry answered.

"The worst is over, Father," Melinda put it. "We're over the mountains, the desert, out of Indian country."

"Every time someone says the worst is over he's proven wrong," Sperry said. "It gets worse when we least expect it."

"I won't let you quit," Melinda said, her voice surprisingly sharp. "You hear me? After what you've put these people through, put yourself through, you can't quit on them and yourself."

"She's right," Cadge Dana put in. "I'd hate to think we've done this for nothing."

"All right. I won't speak of it again," Sperry replied. He didn't, either, but he thought of it a lot as he perched on the rolled red silk of his balloon and watched the river widen and flow southward past prairie and woods and hills.

"Smoke," Cadge Dana said early in the afternoon. The sun was still high, and he stood shading his eyes, looking south. "I see smoke out there, Jessica."

Turning, Jessica saw it too. A thin rising tendril of smoke, gray against the pale sky.

"What does that mean?" Melinda asked.

"Nothing—or anything at all. Indians, soldiers, a settlement. We've got to find out, though."

"Stay away from them, I say," Sperry commented. "We don't need trouble with strangers, not now. It's crazy to risk it."

"About as crazy as drifting on without knowing where we're going," Jessica answered. "I think we ought to find out who that is, and where we are. Don't you, Cadge?"

"Absolutely. We've got to get back on course somehow."

"When we get around this next bend, then. Cadge and I will take a walk over and see what it is. The rest of you stay with the raft. If we don't come back in a reasonable length of time," she added, "go ahead down river."

Jessica borrowed boots from Melinda and took fresh ammunition from her trunk. Cadge armed himself with a Colt .44 and a Winchester repeater. After sweeping around a wide lazy bend in the river, they tied up again, against a bank in the shelter of overhanging cottonwood trees, and Cadge and Jessica waded through shallow water and mud to climb the bank.

It took them only a half-hour's hike to find the source of the smoke. A stone and sod cabin stood alone in the middle of

126

a grassy valley. There was a big oak behind the place, three or four horses wandering the valley, twenty or so longhorns penned up behind the house. A rooster crowed and flapped its wings excitedly as they walked toward the house, and two yapping red dogs rushed out to snap menacingly.

A man with a black beard stepped out from behind the house. Dressed in overalls and a red longjohn shirt, he was the biggest man Jessica had ever seen. Cadge would have measured chest-high on him. He had a corncob pipe in his mouth, a torn flop hat on his head, and a Sharp's rifle in his hands.

From the other corner of the house another of them emerged. Maybe three inches shorter, he still had the measurements of a bear and the dull eyes of a predator.

"I don't like this much," Cadge whispered.

He liked it even less in a minute. The bigger of the two giants raised his rifle to his shoulder and said, "Git!" It was a short speech, but it conveyed enough information.

"We don't want any trouble," Cadge tried. "We just need to know where we are. We're lost."

"Git!" was the response. "Or you're dead."

The front door to the house opened and a woman in calico came out. Her gray hair was tied in a bun. Her weather-lined face framed twinkling blue eyes. She was five feet tall if she was an inch. In her hands was a broom, and she waved it at the giant with the gun.

"Mannerless male! Get out of here, Jake! You got work to do."

"Strangers," the big man mumbled, lowering his head a little.

"Strangers, and so what! Company, I call 'em. Get your brother and get back to that well-digging. Boys!" she said with disgust as the giants ambled off. "Can't teach 'em manners without a rod—and I got a rod to take to 'em, too! Come in now— My, you're a pretty young lady. Come in and set. Mister, you're hurt, aren't you . . ."

Inside, the soddy was clean and neat. The packed earth floor was swept and wildflowers were arranged in a blue-and-white ceramic vase on the mantel above the fireplace.

The woman sat in a rocking chair near the fire and gestured

toward a faded red settee. "Take a load off. Apologize for my boys. Since their daddy died they been like that. Stranger killed my husband, shot him in the face over a mule. Then we had Indians around too. Makes 'em nervous."

They had looked nervous, Jessica thought but didn't say.

"You had Apaches by here?"

"Yes, they was by." The woman rose and pointed to a hole in her paneled wall. "There's a slug nearly got Samuel—he's the baby. What am I thinking of? You folks come a long way, I don't doubt, you'll want food and coffee."

"Not just yet. We have friends down at the river. One wounded seriously. My name is Jessica Starbuck."

"Not up from Texas!"

"Yes."

"Why, Lord, I knew Alex Starbuck as a boy. We lived right on the south border of the Lone Star. Name's Hipple. Don't suppose you recollect it?"

"Yes," Jessica said, "as a matter of fact I do. Amos and Sadie Hipple."

"That's me, Amos is dead, as I told you. I recollect the bad sand-storm year. Alex Starbuck—how is he?" Jessica told him he was dead, and the old woman shook her head. "Sorry, honey. One year, as I was saying, Alex brought down a wagonload of goods for us. It was near Christmas—my babies was hardly more than toddlers. He brought a little sack of fruit and candy for each of 'em. Lord's sake!"

"We'd like to bring our friends up here if we could," Jessica said.

"Of course, honey. I'll have Samuel cut us a roast. I don't get company much . . . Wish I'd have baked an extra pie."

"You're fairly well isolated out here," Cadge said.

"There's no one for thirty miles. Amos got so he couldn't stand people. Some kind of man thing—why do they get like that?" she asked herself. "So we traveled—after the bad dust year—and traveled, and when we got here Amos couldn't see a living soul so he thought 'This must be the place.' Never spoke against it. A wife don't speak against her husband, but God, it was lonely and hard with my two little baby boys."

"Where," Cadge asked, "are we exactly?"

"Mister, you're thirty-one miles exactly from the town of Desperation, which some call it, though they been wanting to change the name to New Empire to bring in more settlers." She muttered, "Old name suits it better."

"If we could, I'd like to borrow a wagon," Jessica said. "To bring our friends up here and perhaps to help us on to Desperation. I'll be happy to pay for the use of it—"

"Don't you say a thing like that," Mrs. Hipple interrupted. "I won't take money from a Starbuck. I'll see that Jake hitches a team." She blinked and asked, "Where exactly did you folks come from, Miz Jessie?"

"We were flying to St. Louis—in a balloon—and we got shot down." The simple woman's face reflected her confusion. "I'll explain it all later."

"All right. We'll eat and you all are going to sleep here. Come morning you take the wagon and do what you have to do. I'll send one of the boys along to bring the wagon back— no," she interrupted Jessica, "don't you dare thank me, Miz Jessie. I owe your daddy, and always wished there was something we could've done to repay him for his kindness. Get along now, get along, and I'll start peeling some potatoes."

Dinner was exceptional and plentiful. The fire blazed away. It was the most comfortable evening they'd had in weeks. Ki was well enough to eat a little and then go to sleep on a down comforter near the fire.

Samuel sat staring at Melinda most of the evening, his eyes glazed by disbelief. After coffee and cake Mrs. Hipple again asked to hear the story of Jessica's travels. She listened with disbelief and occasional horror.

"And that's what that big thing on the wagon is? A floating sky-balloon."

"Yes," Jessica answered. "Exactly that."

"You folks have a lot of courage, I'll say that. But I never heard a thing so astonishing. I can't hardly believe it."

Jake who was standing against the kitchen doorframe, stuffing chocolate cake into his mouth by the handful, said, "I believe it easy, Ma." He wiped his hands on his overalls. "Hell, didn't we see one of them, Samuel?"

The other brother took his eyes off Melinda long enough to

glance at his brother and nod. "We seen 'em."

"You saw us flying? How in the world . . .?"

"Not that balloon, Miz Jessie. Sundown, yesterday. We seen another balloon while we was splittin' wood. Big black-and-white thing just came sailin' over, headin' for Desperation."

★
Chapter 13

On the outskirts of Desperation, which was positioned on a dry plain beside the broad Canadian River, was a brand new sign saying WELCOME TO NEW EMPIRE. Jake Hipple, driving the wagon, snorted derisively.

Ki was sitting up in the back of the wagon, his back against the rolled silk. Melinda was leaning her head against his shoulder. He showed no sign of infection and had no fever—both good signs. At breakfast, Ki, who usually had tea and toast if he had anything, had wolfed down two slices of ham and four eggs, followed by half a pitcher of milk.

"No sign of the balloon," Sperry said, meaning Gregor's black-and-white behemoth.

Jessica, seated between Jake and the professor, said, "He must have flown right over."

Sperry wasn't so sure. "He would need repairs too. We saw him go down when the lightning struck the balloon. I don't know how they made it this far, but whatever temporary repairs they could have made in the mountains wouldn't carry them far."

"You think they're here?" Jake asked.

"I think," Sperry answered, "they are here."

"Want some help? I know most of the boys around town. We can string 'em up or catch 'em in an alley."

"No, thank you, Jake," Jessica said, putting a hand briefly on Jake's wrist, watching as he blushed to the roots of his hair. "But it's kind of you. It's our battle."

"Don't look like you got many warriors left," Jake said, nodding toward the bed of the wagon where the injured Cadge

131

Dana perched next to the newly wounded Ki.

"It'll be all right." Her hand fell from his wrist, but she smiled brightly, causing Jake to blush even deeper. The big man looked away deliberately and hurried the team on toward the small town.

Jake dropped them behind the hotel and helped unload the balloon. Then, regretfully it seemed, he started back toward the ranch.

"First thing?" Melinda asked.

"Get a room for Ki and put him to bed."

"Hardly necessary, Jessica," Ki said.

"It's necessary. Besides, there's nothing you can do just now."

"Unless Gregor is in town," he pointed out.

"There's still little you could do," Jessica said, tapping her own shoulder meaningfully.

"You have such little faith in me." Ki slid from the wagon and stood, swaying slightly. Melinda escorted him through the back door of the big red building as the others waited.

"Did you see any sort of dry goods store, a ladies' dress shop?" Sperry asked. "We need silk."

"Won't something else do, just for a patch?" Dana asked.

"Yes, I suppose so. We need a carpenter too, and we'll have to purchase some good manila line."

"Those shouldn't present any problem, even in a town the size of Desperation."

"New Empire," Cadge corrected.

"All right, even in New Empire. We'll have to split up and have a look around, I guess. Should've asked Jake about a carpenter. Can you give me some sort of a figure, Professor, on how much weight we can handle? It'll likely have to be built out of two by fours."

"I'll try and calculate it, yes."

"Maybe even a quick sketch of the dimensions."

"Yes, no problem. But we are losing time, much time. I fear we've already lost this race."

Cadge said, "From here on, barring weather problems, it's a pretty easy trip, isn't it?"

"Barring weather problems," Jessica answered. "And saboteurs."

By the time Melinda had gotten Ki settled in his room and returned, her father had sketched out a gondola much smaller than the original one, but which he thought workable.

"Now to find a carpenter who will drop everything he's doing and build it. Today."

"Is this an inducement?" Sperry asked, handing over his money belt.

"The best there is," Jessica answered. "But I'll take care of the cost, Professor Sperry. Keep that in reserve."

Cadge and Jessica went looking for a hammer-and-saw man, while the Professor and Melinda searched for a dry-goods store. Asking people on the street, Jessie and Cadge were directed to the south end of town, where two men were nailing up a joist for the ceiling of a new building.

"Hey!" Jessie called up.

"What do you want, lady?" the man with the red face yelled down.

"I want to hire you."

"Fine! Come around tomorrow before eight and we'll talk about it. We got a job right now, and Judge Hawkins is in a mighty big hurry for us to finish it."

"Is there anyone else around who's not working?"

"Nope," the man said impatiently, driving nails again.

"How much are you making by the day?" Jessie shouted above the din.

Sighing, the older carpenter stopped hammering and said, "Something like two-fifty a day for me an' my kid here."

"I'll pay you a hundred to take the day off."

"What did you say?"

"A hundred. Is that enough?"

The two carpenters looked at each other and then started down the ladder. Jessie slipped them five gold pieces, showed them the professor's plan.

"What is this?" the carpenter asked, scratching his head. "It's either the smallest cabin I ever seen or the biggest dog house."

Jessie explained as the carpenters, father and son, exchanged skeptical glances. "It has to be as light as possible. What materials you use aren't important—here's another fifty dollars to buy what you need."

"It's gonna go up in the air, is it?"

"That's about it."

"Okay, tell me what you think of a plank floor—nice kiln-dried pine—frame it up and make these sides here out of canvas. That'll save you a lot of weight."

"Fine. So long as it holds together."

The carpenter was aggrieved. "Lady, what Art Schofield builds stays built."

"Fine. The rest of the balloon is behind the hotel in the stubble field. If you can build it there it would help considerably."

"We can build it anywhere you want for this money. 'Sides, Judge Hawkins likely won't find us there."

That settled, Jessie and Cadge went off to find Sperry and Melinda. They walked down the dusty main street of the community, which apparently was growing. Besides the job they had just left, there was an evidently new emporium, still unpainted, and three saloons, all with many horses tied in front.

The jailhouse was of stone, the courthouse next door of red brick. "They might make it yet," Jessie commented.

Cadge didn't respond to that. Instead, the big blond reporter said, "You know we're being followed, don't you?"

"I saw them."

"Tyler Gregor's men?"

"I don't know. You don't recognize them from San Francisco?" Jessica asked.

"No. And I haven't seen Gregor, but I'm keeping my eyes open."

"Stop in here," Jessica said, nodding at the Emporium Deluxe, as it was called.

Cadge looked in the window. "The professor's not in there."

"Cadge," Jessie swept her hands down her thighs. "I have got to buy some clothes. These are Melinda's. Mine are back along the river—probably some Indian is wearing them by now. The boots hurt my feet, the pants are too tight."

"All right!" Dana held up a defensive hand and laughed. "Sorry." He looked up the street and said, "I'll hang around here and see if anyone we know comes by."

Cadge settled onto a green-painted bench next to a white-bearded, dozing man, and studied the passing traffic as Jessie ducked inside the emporium. He saw nothing, no one, and began to wonder if their imagination was playing tricks on them, making them see murderers and saboteurs everywhere. It wouldn't have been surprising considering what they had been through.

Now Cadge, warmed by the sunlight, did begin composing his series of articles about the journey, in his head. He again debated with himself about the wisdom of not telling Jessica and Ki all he suspected about the events of the last week, but again he followed his newsman's instincts and decided to keep silent.

Jessie emerged from the store with a brown-paper-wrapped package half an hour later and they started looking for Melinda and Sperry. They could hear hammering behind the hotel. Schofield hadn't wasted any time getting started.

The dry-goods store across from the stable was new, yellow, well-stocked for this section of the territory. They found Melinda and the professor inside, Melinda idly examining the goods on the shelves, the professor at the counter facing a stout, blue-frocked woman with her hair coiled on top of her head.

"Yes, I've got silk," the woman was whining. "But it was a special order for the mayor's wife. Her daughter's getting married. All the wedding gowns are to be cut from that."

"We don't need a lot; half a bolt will do."

"I *told* you, I already sold half a bolt to the other man— Lord, I'm down to the line now. One wrong cut and one of the bridesmaids will have to wear burlap."

Jessica walked that way, giving her own package to Dana to hold. "I realize you have a problem," Jessie said quietly, offering the clerk her best smile, "but so do we." Three gold pieces, double eagles, had somehow found their way onto the counter top. "You're obviously a resourceful woman. Surely you can find some way to cut corners." Three more double-eagles had reached the counter. The lady's eyes were bulging with avarice.

"She'll kill me. Mr. Hammaker will kill me . . ." she said,

135

as she brought out a bolt of blue silk and started cutting it.

"We'll need a dozen spools of thread, too," Melinda said. "The color doesn't matter. Whatever you've been trying to sell for a long while and haven't."

"There's that awful fuchsia . . ."

"Fine."

Cadge had sidled up to the counter. "These other men who wanted silk—can you describe them?"

"What? I don't know. They hadn't shaven for a while," she said with a sniff of contempt. "Rough men. Their leader had a narrow face, a longish dark mustache and eyes I didn't care for . . ." She blushed. "It was like he was mentally undressing me."

Looking at the woman, Cadge was dubious, but the description matched Tyler Gregor well enough for him to glance at Jessie and mutter, "Trouble for sure. We weren't wrong."

"What is it?" the professor asked, but this wasn't the place to fill him in. Cadge just shook his head as the nervous but obviously satisfied clerk handed over their parcel.

Jessica went up to see Ki in his hotel room and found the convalescent dressing. She watched him silently from the doorway. Then she said, "You're going to kill yourself."

"No, lying in bed is the killing thing." He winced as he tried to shoulder into his shirt, and Jessica went to help him.

"You need rest."

"We'll be leaving soon, won't we? I'll have to get up anyway. A little food, tea if I can find some, and I'll be ready." Ki asked, "You didn't expect me to stay behind, did you, Jessie?"

"Not hardly. Unless we tied you down."

"Well then . . ." Ki slipped into his vest and pulled his slippers on, all of it taking more effort than he would have believed.

"Gregor is in town," Jessie revealed. Ki's eyes altered. He turned slowly toward her.

"You are sure?"

"Reasonably sure. We haven't seen the balloon, but a man matching his description bought silk at the dry-goods store. And someone's been keeping an eye on us."

"I don't like that. The man is a killer."

"There's not much we can do about it at this point," Jessica pointed out.

Ki wasn't quite so sure. "If we could locate his balloon, we might be able to do something."

"I don't want you getting any crazy ideas, Ki. You're not well enough to go out making war, and you know it."

"Wait until he decides to make war on us again—is that it?"

"No, that's not it, and you know it. Just don't get these ideas in your head, Ki."

But the idea was already firmly rooted in Ki's mind. He didn't argue with Jessica; she was only trying to protect him. Ki was only thinking of protecting all of them against a gang of high-flying murderers.

With Jessica he went out of the hotel and found the carpenters still hard at work on the gondola. Just now, they were tacking canvas around the framework of the device. Melinda, opening and clenching her right hand, came up to them.

"My fingers are frozen," she said. "All that sewing . . ."

"You have the patches on?" Ki asked.

"Yes." She looked at Ki, noting the thinness of his face, the rings below his eyes. "You sure you should be up and around?" she asked.

"Again?" Ki laughed. "The two of you should have been nurses. I'm all right, yes. For the last time."

"Father has the burner adjusted," Melinda said, still fixing a dubious stare at Ki. "When the gondola's finished we'll be ready to reattach it and start inflating. The lines are as good as ever, probably better. We found another one that had been cut by rifle fire—it's a wonder that one didn't snap and put us down for good."

"How long would you say before we're ready to take off?" Ki asked. Jessica looked at him with suspicion. He had an idea in his head and wasn't going to drop it.

"An hour—an hour and a half," Melinda responded.

"I see." Ki stretched his good arm. "I think I'll take a walk and try to wake up a little."

"Not alone," Jessica said firmly.

137

"I'll go with him," Melinda put in.

Ki looked uncomfortable, Jessica noted. She could read his mind like a book. He wanted to go out and scout around for Gregor, and he wanted to do it alone. He refused to take Jessica along, but she reasoned that Melinda was just as good an escort. He wouldn't do anything to threaten the redhead.

Melinda took Ki's arm, and they went off together, Ki scowling back at Jessie.

"What was the matter with Jessica?" Melinda asked as they walked through a back alley toward the main street of Desperation.

"I didn't notice that anything was wrong," Ki answered.

"Sure you did. Come clean, Ki."

"You know Gregor is around town, don't you?"

"I know they suspect it."

"Jessica thinks I want to start off on some vendetta against him. She doesn't think I'm capable of it just now."

"Well?" Melinda laughed and squeezed his arm.

"I may not be capable of it," Ki answered quietly, although the way he said it made it perfectly clear that *he* thought he was, "but it can never hurt to know where the enemy is, how he is armed, what his intentions are."

"And I'm the leash?" Melinda asked. At Ki's questioning glance she expanded her observation. "I'm supposed to keep you out of trouble. So that the poor little girl doesn't get hurt, I'm along to prevent you from trying anything foolish."

Ki admitted, "That seems to be Jessica's thought."

"Well?" She stopped as they came out of the mouth of the alley. A beer wagon rolled past, its big Belgian horses churning the roadway to mud.

"Well what?"

"You think we ought to find them, don't you? So do I. They want to kill us, don't they, Ki? Bunch of bastards. Let's have our look around."

"It is dangerous," Ki said.

"Ki," the redhead said, her blue eyes searching his, "what hasn't been dangerous since San Francisco?"

Ki hesitated, but finally he nodded. "All right. We can at

138

least look around and find out where Gregor's men are and possibly what they're up to."

"No wars, Ki?"

"No wars."

But it wasn't something you could promise someone. Peace takes agreement on both sides. Gregor hadn't offered an olive branch yet, and the odds were he wouldn't. As they noted, Gregor was liable for criminal charges and, especially with Cadge Dana's press connections, he stood every chance of facing those charges unless he succeeded in eliminating the witnesses against him.

They asked a barefoot boy with a fishing pole and three large catfish, "Seen anything of some men with a big balloon?"

"Why?" the boy asked defensively.

Ki flashed a silver dollar, which answered all objections in the kid's mind. He caught it on the fly as Ki flipped it to him and then pointed. "Seen 'em across the little creek. Good cats up along there," he said, hoisting his to demonstrate.

"Thank you," Ki said.

The kid dashed off with his prize fish and prized dollar, and Ki and Melinda started on. She saw him finger a *shuriken* in his vest pocket and reminded him, "No war."

"I wouldn't think of it."

They walked slowly through the trees like two wandering lovers, and found the site where Tyler Gregor was trying to patch his lightning-torn balloon together.

There was only one man watching the aircraft and Melinda saw Ki's eyebrows draw together, his body tense.

"Easy now," she cautioned.

"Easy is the only way," Ki replied, yet his pulse had lifted, his breathing slowed, his eyes focused sharply. One man! Gregor would be in town collecting supplies or hiring crafts-men, perhaps having a drink or two with his people, even spying on Sperry as he prepared his balloon.

There was one man here—armed with a shotgun, it was true, but still a single man—and what single man was a match for Ki, wounded or not.

"Ki," Melinda whispered, "you're worrying me—the look in your eyes . . ."

"I want you to stay right here." Ki took Melinda by the hands and looked directly into her eyes. "You understand me, Melinda? Right here."

"And you . . . ?"

"I am going to do exactly what you think," Ki answered.

He didn't wait for an answer. He let her hands drop. "Wait here, Melinda, please."

"Ki—" Her protest was little more than a whimper that broke off into angry silence.

Ki moved through the shadows cast by the trees, crossed the creek at a rocky ford, and moved up behind the balloon. The silk was spread across the earth, still attached to the gondola, which appeared to be undamaged.

The single guard walked slowly back and forth, kicking at pebbles and twigs on the ground, obviously disgusted with this duty. He was swarthy and short, wearing loose-fitting trousers and a blue army jacket.

He never saw Ki. He felt the forearm go around his throat and struggled for a moment, but then he slumped into unconsciousness. Ki didn't bother to hide the man. He simply cast his weapons away and then climbed aboard the gondola.

It was made of bamboo and was large—not as large as Sperry's had been, but large enough for a crew of six. Ki's first thought was of the burner, but he decided to poke around a little first. Glancing up the road to town he saw no one coming, so he moved on into the first room he came to, a storage bin. There was a lock on the door, but the bamboo splintered and gave easily, and Ki was inside.

Rifles, a fuel drum, provisions. No mail sack.

Suppose Gregor *had* no mail sack? Suppose Ki slipped off with it? It was as effective as destroying the burner—more so, perhaps.

Ki went out of the storeroom and entered the next cabin. There was a sextant in there, thrown on a light cot, and a spare compass. More rifles and two shotguns hanging on wall clips. Gregor had planned for a war, it seemed.

The mail sack was under the bunk.

140

It was identical in appearance to the one on Sperry's craft, but there *was* a difference. Ki hefted it and frowned. It was heavy, very much heavier than the one on their own airship.

Crouching, he slashed a small rent in the canvas sack and groped inside. There was no mail of the ordinary sort, only numbers of small, oilskin-wrapped bundles.

Frowning, Ki pulled one through the cut he had made and unwrapped the package. A black and tarry lump of material was inside. Ki tasted it and then spat it out. It was very bitter, and Ki knew what it was.

He had seen opium before.

The woman's scream interrupted Ki's investigation. A chill ran up his spine and his mind turned over, blurring all thoughts but one. They had Melinda.

Chapter 14

Ki was on deck and over the rail in seconds. He leaped to the ground, landed wrong, and felt jagged pain rip through his shoulder. He ignored the pain and began running toward the creek. Melinda screamed again before he could reach it.

Stupid, he told himself. Stupid to let the woman accompany him. She wasn't Jessica Starbuck, had no fighting skills, carried no weapon. She was simply a scientist's daughter.

Through the trees Ki saw a man's figure. Something was said, but he couldn't catch it. They didn't see him yet, and by the time they did it was too late.

One-armed, Ki was a match for the two men who had Melinda. They were pawing at her, trying to tear her blouse off. A leaping *tobi-geri* kick jerked the first man's head back and slammed him to the ground. Landing lightly, Ki spun, side-kicked the second thug, driving him back, and then moved in again, driving a stunning *yonhon-nukite* blow into the man's diaphragm before finishing him with a chopping blow to the neck.

Melinda was shaken; tears filmed her eyes. She was trying to tug her blouse together as she stared at the downed thugs.

"Ki!" She was in his arms then, finding a safe sanctuary from the world in the strong warrior who held her, smiled down at her, and hugged her with his good arm.

"We don't want to stay around here," Ki said.

"No. Ki—are they dead?"

He looked at the two men on the ground. Whether they were or not was really a matter of indifference to him. He didn't bother to check.

"No," he told her, since that was what she wanted to hear. "They aren't dead, Melinda."

"They're Gregor's men . . .? What did you find, what did you do?"

"We'll talk later. We don't want to be here if anyone else shows up. Let's get that balloon in the air and clear out."

"Yes." She turned, Ki's arm still around her shoulders. "You're right."

The balloon was lifting its crimson crown above the hotel roof by the time they returned. The gondola was in place, although the carpenters were making a few last hasty modifications.

Jessica came out to meet them. She saw the state of Melinda's clothing, the hard look in Ki's eyes, the fresh blood seeping through his shirt at the shoulder.

"Ki, what happened?"

"Not now, please, Jessica. Let's get on board. How long before we lift off?"

"Minutes, if we're in a hurry."

"We are," Ki said, "in a hurry."

The carpenters, a little richer and still slightly dazed, backed away from the gondola as Cadge, Jessie, Ki, and Melinda scrambled aboard. No one had to tell Sperry that something was up—it was written all over them. He opened the burner wide, and the flame jutted upward with a whoosh. Then he motioned to Cadge to start bringing in the mooring lines.

In fifteen minutes they were aloft again, following the river toward the Texas line. Ki had his shoulder looked at, and Melinda slipped into one of Jessie's new cotton shirts.

When they were well under way Ki called a conference. He looked first at Cadge, who was crouched against the floor of the new gondola, his light hair blowing in the wind.

"You were right, Dana," Ki told him.

"Right?" Cadge was all innocence.

"You knew there was something else to this jaunt but just a balloon race. I assume you also knew what it was. Now I do. I was on board Gregor's balloon today."

"I don't seem to know what you mean," Cadge said evasively. It was obvious that he did know something, however.

"The opium," Ki said straight out.

"That . . ." Cadge shrugged. "Well, I thought that was it. There wasn't any proof, but that was my guess."

"What are you two talking about?" Jessica asked, looking from one man to the other.

"The mail sack Tyler Gregor is carrying doesn't have a letter in it, Jessie, not a postcard. It's crammed full of opium. Cadge knew about this, but he wouldn't say a word. It explains why Gregor is so intent on stopping us—he wanted to stop Cadge, isn't that right?"

"Could be," Dana admitted.

"Cadge," Jessica said, touching his wrist. "It's time now to tell us about it, don't you think?"

"Yes." He smiled. "Past time, I suppose. A good reporter doesn't want to leak his scoop before he's proven it. You have to understand that. I didn't mean to endanger anyone—I expect he would have done just what he did anyway."

Melinda shook her head. "I *still* don't know what everyone is talking about. Opium?"

"It's been one of Tyler Gregor's sidelines for a long while. Ship's crews from the Orient inevitably pay a visit to Gregor's Barbary Coast saloon."

"He's a drug runner?"

"A peddler at least—I don't know who's the top dog. Or . . . I didn't. I had a few pointers, hints here and there."

"Now you know?" Melinda asked.

"Of course. Gustav Schultz. There's a large Chinese population in St. Louis. That's where the market for opium has always been, among the Chinese. Not long ago two separate shipments of opium were intercepted. Two wagonloads, found quite by chance. Schultz decided, apparently, that the authorities were clamping down, that taking the opium overland was inviting trouble."

"Hence the grand idea," Jessica said.

"Hence the grand idea. A delivery by balloon. Gregor is a former circus man, and he's got a lot of imagination. *Fly* the dope to St. Louis. And keep flying it. There's no marshal in the sky. The event was too public a spectacle for anyone to suspect it for what it was. And the fifty-thousand-dollar prize appeared to be reason enough for a thug like Gregor to be involved."

"*That* was what you didn't want to tell us all along?" Melinda inquired.

"That's it."

"But . . . didn't you trust us?"

"Melinda," Cadge said soberly, "for all I knew you and your father were drug runners as well. The whole fleet might have been carrying opium to St. Louis."

"How could you think that!"

"After you agreed to take a reporter along, I didn't anymore, not really. Still, I couldn't be certain."

"You haven't told us the last bit yet," Jessica Starbuck said.

"Oh?" Cadge's grin was nearly feline. "You're a difficult woman to conceal things from, Jessie."

"I'm lost again," Melinda admitted.

"I've seen a lot of cagey reporters, and some who were willing to risk their lives for a story," Jessica explained, "but *this* man does go to extraordinary lengths."

"All right," Cadge said. He turned up the bottom of the yellow sweater he was wearing. The brass badge shone dully. "State of California" was all Melinda read before he folded the sweater down again.

"Then why don't we just have them arrested?" Melinda asked. "You can do that. You could have done it back in Desperation, or even before."

"Because," Ki said, "Gregor and his men wouldn't talk and Cadge would still have no firm evidence that our brewer, Gustav Schultz, was the kingpin of the drug operation."

"Yes, I didn't think of that," Melinda admitted. "But now, if they know who you are, and they know that Ki has stumbled onto the opium, we're in worse trouble than ever, aren't we? I mean, they can't let us live, none of us."

"No, they can't," Dana said. "But I don't think they know who I am, and with any luck they may not know that Ki found anything on their gondola. They might just think we're trying to fight back and win that fifty thousand dollars."

145

His reassurance did no good. "Either way," Melinda said, "they want us dead."

"Either way," Cadge greed, "they want us dead."

The Staked Plains, long and dry, passed beneath the balloon as they reached the Texas border and sailed on toward Missouri. They weren't alone. They had spotted the big black-and-white-striped balloon behind them an hour earlier.

"Too bad I didn't have ten minutes more on their ship," Ki said to Jessica. "I could have finished this."

"It wouldn't have finished a thing," Jessie argued. At Ki's curious glance she said, "If the balloon went down for good and all, what would Gregor do? Transfer the opium to a wagon and take it on into St. Louis, ruining a hundred more lives. No, Ki, the only real solution now is to finish Tyler Gregor and his men forever. If Cadge can't arrest them, then —we'll take care of them."

"That won't eliminate Schultz. Cadge is right; we just about have to let them make the connection."

"That leaves us as sitting ducks," Jessica Starbuck said.

"If they start shooting again, we'll have to do our best to protect ourselves. If they leave us alone, we'll let them go through to St. Louis."

"They can't let us go through, Ki, can they?"

Ki didn't answer. He shrugged and returned to his project —loading an eight-gauge shotgun with glass and nails. If the two balloons engaged in combat again, Ki meant to be ready this time. Cadge Dana and Schultz be damned—there was no way Ki was going to let the balloon carrying Jessie and Melinda go down.

"Getting dark," Cadge said, as he approached Ki, silently noting his work. "We'll have to set down. Know where we are?"

"Only roughly," Ki answered.

"I thought you two were from Texas," Cadge said.

"Somehow," Ki told the lawman drily, "I've never gotten around to memorizing all two hundred and sixty-seven thousand square miles of this parcel of land."

"Sorry."

"As near as I can figure we're drifting toward the Red

146

River, perhaps within twenty miles of Fort Sill—just a guess. Bad country in the old days—Comanche country, but they've drifted out of the area for the most part."

"Gregor seems closer yet," Cadge commented.

"Yes, he does. He's going to grow more desperate, Cadge. More desperate and yet more cautious. If he doesn't take us out pretty soon, he knows his number's up. But he also knows we're onto him."

"So what does he do, Ki?"

"I wish we knew," Ki said, squinting into the sunset at their constant, deadly companion. "I only wish we knew."

"No more raids on his camp, I take it?"

"He'll be expecting it, be totally prepared. No—that course of action is out."

"Then?"

"Then we wait for him to make a move," Ki said. "That's all we can do."

They set down on a vast plain that night. There seemed to be no horizon. The land stretching so far into the vast Texas distances was becoming as dark as the sky.

They built a fire, disregarding the limited risk it carried to do so. The big Texas sky was flooded with bright stars. After eating, Cadge asked Jessie to go out walking in the time-honored Southwestern way.

With his arm around her small waist, Cadge strolled with her, counting stars, his hip bumping against hers with each step.

They stopped and he turned her toward him, kissing her moist, parted lips as she rubbed his back, leaning against him so that the weight and warmth of her breasts was too palpable, too stimulating.

He slowly unbuttoned her blouse, letting his lips follow his fingers downward, tasting her smooth flesh, teasing her nipples with his tongue as Jessie rested her hands on his head. Tugging her blouse from her jeans, she slipped from it and tossed it aside to stand like a half-naked goddess in the starlight. Cadge's eager hands moved across her breasts and then dropped to the waistband of her jeans, trying to squeeze their way downward.

147

"Just a minute," Jessica said. She slipped from her jeans and boots and stood smiling before him, naked and proud and beautiful.

Cadge stripped his clothing in a flat minute and moved against her, his erection against her belly. She took it in both hands and toyed with it gently, cupping his sack as she did so.

Then, with a single light movement, she had her legs wrapped around Cadge's waist and she had slipped him inside her already wet, accommodating body.

She let her arms drape over his shoulders as he caressed her smooth, firm butt and let his fingers trail down the crack to touch her from behind.

Jessie smiled and nudged him with her pelvis, drawing his thick, solid shaft in and out as she kissed his ear and neck, her breath warm and teasing against his flesh.

She nipped him on the ear and Cadge flinched. "What was that for?" he asked.

"For not trusting us and telling us about the opium."

"Look, Jessica—"

"End of discussion," she said, and as her warm body wrapped itself around his, swaying and pulsing with life, it was. Cadge couldn't remember the conversation fifteen seconds later.

His concentration was focused on the need rising inside him, the shaking of his leg, the thrust of Jessie's body against his, the press of her breasts and her whispered urgings.

When he came it was sudden and hard, and he almost staggered back to fall against the grass. Jessica, smiling deeply, stroking his forehead, continued to move against him, the warmth of her incredible, until she too climaxed, clinging to Cadge Dana as she trembled and leaned back her head to make a deeply pleasured sound. She stared up at the night stars as he turned her in a slow lazy circle.

"All right," she said. "I forgive you."

Cadge had no idea what she meant; he only knew that the night was good, but unfortunately growing colder. They stepped back into their clothing and walked arm in arm back to the camp where the low fire had nearly burned itself out.

* * *

148

Morning was clear and bright above the plains. The wind was northeasterly, as Sperry had predicted, and it carried them on across the Panhandle and over Indian territory. There was no sign of the other balloon—but no one believed Gregor had given it up.

"We've got enough of a lead that I don't think he can catch up now," Melinda said. "Do you, Ki?"

"I think he *has* to catch up," Ki answered. "He has to finish us now, Melinda."

"Unless he flies at night . . ."

"In this country," Ki said, his arm sweeping over the flat, empty land, "why not?"

"You think we should try it too, don't you?"

Ki shrugged. "If we can, for as long as we can. The trouble now is that only your father knows how to properly operate the burner and he is growing more exhausted with each day. You can see it in his eyes, around the mouth."

"I don't think he really understood how much energy this would require. He's not a physical man and he believes he is capable of doing whatever his mind envisions, forgetting that the body can only carry on for so long."

"Cadge can operate it to an extent. Perhaps it would be best if Dana handled things until nightfall, let your father have a little more rest—then make a decision at sunset."

"What are you two talking about?" Cadge asked. When they told him he said, "I'm willing. Funny—I'd almost like to see the bastard catch up. See what a shotgun-load of glass and nails would do to that balloon, right, Ki?"

"Possibly, but you can bet Gregor has taken extra precautions now. His men will be armed and ready and they'll start shooting the minute they see us. With the women, I don't relish another battle in the sky. Nor," Ki said frankly, "do I look forward to possibly going down. On the ground I feel confident at all times. Here . . . who knows what can happen, Cadge."

Sperry didn't like to give up the helm, if it could be called that. He didn't want to rest, and he certainly didn't want to fly all night, but he was as aware of any of them that Tyler Gregor was a killer, a desperate man, and in the end he went along with their suggestion.

Ki stripped off his shirt and stood rubbing the flesh around his torn shoulder. It itched like mad now. It was healing, but it was difficult to say if the pain was harder to endure than the itching or not.

Jessica asked him, "Well, do we believe Cadge Dana?"

One eyebrow lifted and Ki turned toward her with surprise. "Why, don't you?"

"*I* do, yes, at a certain level, an instinctual one, but logic still tells me everything he's told us might not be true."

"We found the opium, Jessica."

"Yes, but he didn't mention it until after you discovered it. Thinking about it, you'd think Cadge, the authorities, could have notified the St. Louis police to pick up Gregor when he lands there. Why fly along with us?"

"Cadge is a maverick. I suspect he wanted to do it on his own. Maybe he's still trying to protect his cover as a newsman. I don't know, Jessica—have you asked him?"

"Not exactly."

Ki smiled. "You haven't done too well interrogating Cadge Dana, have you?"

"Something," Jessica said, leaning on the rail, "always seems to happen when I try."

The wind was fresh all day and into evening, pushing them back toward the north and east, up toward St. Louis, still beyond the rest of Indian territory and the entire state of Missouri. Night fell and they decided to go on despite the hazards. Jessica lit a lamp below, and, besides the stars, it was the only light in the dark world of the plains.

Melinda had been looking through the provisions, counting their goods and estimating the length of time they had before St. Loius. "It'll be close," she decided, "but at least there's enough water. We may be able to make it through without setting down again—thank God. It seems every time we set down something awful happens."

"And," Cadge said, stretching after his day's work hunkered over the temperamental burner, "every time we ascend something happens. Anyone know of a convenient place in between?"

"I see a light," Ki said almost under his breath.

150

"What?"

"I see a light behind us. There, a little to the north."

"Venus? A low star?" Melinda asked, but as they stood looking at the light in the distance they already, each of them, knew full well what it was. Who it was.

Chapter 15

The lamp went out and they drifted on the night wind beneath ten million stars, watching the flickering distant light behind them. "They're not gaining," Melinda said, but it was more a hopeful statement than one of fact—no one could tell if Tyler Gregor was indeed gaining or falling behind. "With the morning, we'll begin to fly over more populated areas."

"I don't think that's going to trouble Tyler Gregor one way or the other," Dana said.

Sunrise was a pale band of red along the eastern horizon followed by the sudden glare of the sun. Below them they spotted scattered farms now, here and there a small community, long cornfields and small herds of livestock.

"They'll spot us now, against the sunrise."

"Still back there?" Jessica asked.

"What did you expect?" Cadge was as grim as Jessica had ever seen him. "They'll be around. Maybe we'd better check the weapons again. Ki?"

"I think so." Ki was scanning the darker western skies, like Cadge, expecting nothing but what he eventually saw. It was a thousand feet above them but descending, looking bigger and more menacing than ever. Tyler Gregor's aircraft, guns bristling, was zeroing in on them.

"The guns, quickly," Ki said, although he hardly had to remind anybody that there was little time to waste. Tyler, in a nearly suicidal maneuver, had let much hot air out of his balloon; it was sinking like a stone toward them and before Ki had finished his last admonition, a rifle from above spoke, a bullet clipping the lumber of the gondola.

152

Cadge, moving in a crouch, tossed Ki the lethally loaded eight-gauge shotgun. Then he went to the rail and without waiting for further provocation opened up with his Henry repeater, sending a hail of lead toward the downward-swooping balloon manned by the opium runners.

Jessie could hear the odd snapping sound as rifle bullets punctured the silk of their balloon. Kneeling at the rail she brought her Colt .38 up and gave them some of their own back.

A man stood up, grabbed at his throat and then fell, cartwheeling through space. He didn't miss their gondola by thirty feet.

"Ki!" Cadge Dana shouted as he saw the man in a white duster level a shotgun at their silk. Ki put his own scattergun to his shoulder, drew back both hammers, and touched off.

The roar in his ears was astonishing as the eight-gauge sent its load of glass and nails into Tyler Gregor's silk. Both shotguns had been fired at once and even as Ki took the tremendous jolt to his shoulder produced by his own weapon, he saw flame jut from the muzzles of the Gregor scattergun, heard a dull thump overhead, and felt the gondola careen.

Gregor's balloon, already dropping at a rapid pace, sped past them as the gaping hole Ki's thunder gun had torn in the silk sent it into a spinning dive.

Ki watched it fall away for a moment and then just held on—there wasn't any choice. They were going down again and no amount of effort, no prayer, was going to slow their descent.

The river was wide and silver in the morning light and when they hit it they hit it hard. The gondola immediately started sinking and Ki dove overboard, treading water as he looked back for the others.

Jessica was beyond the gondola, which the wind was dragging across the river. Melinda was just now deserting the craft. Sperry was perched on top of the gondola yet and they yelled for him to dive. Finally he went feet-first into the water and began paddling toward shore.

There was no sign of Cadge for a moment. Then he bobbed up near Ki, shaking his hair from his eyes. "Caught in a damn

153

line," he sputtered, spitting out water. "Jessica?"

"She's all right. Can you swim, Cadge?"

"Yeah. See where Gregor went down?"

"No, I didn't." Ki started stroking toward the far shore. It seemed impossibly distant, and his wounded shoulder didn't help any. Finally he dragged himself up on the beach to sit, breathing deeply, arms around his legs. Melinda lay flat on her back next to her father, who was shaking with cold and exhaustion. Jessica and Cadge were leaning against each other, as if that was the only way they could remain sitting up.

"Should someone say congratulations?" Cadge asked hoarsely.

Jessica looked at him as if he'd lost his mind. "What are you talking about, Cadge?"

"Unless there's another monster like that on this continent, we've just crossed the Mississippi River—not that we wanted to. And that means we're in Illinois. It also means that somewhere fifty, a hundred miles north of us—take your own guess—is St. Louis, Missouri."

"The balloon," Melinda pointed out, "is still in the water, the silk blown apart."

"That's right," Cadge said, lifting his eyes to look at the red silk floating three-quarters deflated on the water. "What do you say we get it ashore? Ki? What are we sitting around for?"

"Can it fly again, Professor Sperry?" Jessica wanted to know. The scientist shook his head wearily in answer.

"Patch it again, rebuild the gondola again, fly again . . . I don't know. I've just about given up hope."

"Not now," Jessica said, walking to the old man to crouch down before him. "Don't give it up now—we're so near."

"I don't know if it's possible. The burner doused, the fabric ripped."

"We can get it to shore and have a look, right, Ki?"

"Yes, we can at least do that." Studying Sperry's face, though, Ki could see the fight had gone out of the man completely. No wonder—a man nearly sixty, sedentary, involved in gunbattles, sabotage, a hair-raising fall into the river. He was cold, hungry, tired, and seemed to want nothing more than cover up his face and shut out the world.

154

Ki said, "Come on, Professor. This is just the first step. How are we ever going to get to the moon?"

Sperry smiled weakly. "I wonder if I'd have to fight my way all the way there as well. All right—" A little strength seemed to come back into him as he got to his feet. "Let's assess the damage and see what can be done." He looked to the far shore of the vast river. "Will they...?"

"I don't think they're going to be able to get in the air again, not after Ki blasted that silk," Dana said.

"There's no reason why they should even try," Jessica said. "They can find a few horses and ride into St. Louis with their cargo."

"That doesn't help us much, does it?" Melinda commented. "They still have to take care of us, don't they, Ki? If they can— They still have to try to kill us."

Ki didn't answer. He hugged her once and then went with Dana to see what could be done about dragging the balloon, which had snagged itself on some broken riverside brush, to shore.

"Mad dreams," Sperry muttered, and Jessie, with color in her cheeks, tried to snap him out of it.

"You've proved that it was absolutely *not* a mad dream, Dr. Sperry. Look how far you've come, the lessons we've learned. The only reason things went so badly is because we had *killers* behind us all the way from San Francisco! You've shown the world that flights like this are possible. That's why none of us can stand to hear you talk of giving it up now!"

"You're right," Sperry said weakly. "You are absolutely right, young lady." He threw back his shoulders, wiped at his hair with a trembling hand, and said, "This in itself is a victory, isn't it? This in itself. Let's see if we can't help our young men with the balloon."

They finally dragged the rig ashore, but the damage was even worse than any of them had expected. Let alone the twisted, shattered gondola, the balloon's fabric itself was shredded in half a dozen places, some of the gaps very large. The silk was wet, incapable of true inflation if it had been sound. The burner would have to be taken apart, dried out, and reassembled.

"How long?" Jessica asked. Sperry, looking unhappier than ever, answered softly.

"Who can tell—a day, two? If we had anything to work with—the toolbox is gone, we have no silk, no needle and thread, the fuel is probably contaminated by water . . ."

"Then," Jessica said brightly, "we'd better start planning how to go about it."

"It's impossible!"

"Fifteen-hundred miles was impossible. Fifty more isn't." Jessica said convincingly. "Do you want that fifty thousand dollars or not? Do you need it or not? Do you want the recognition that will come for having achieved this? Make up your mind, Professor Sperry. We're all with you still. If you want us to give up too, then we will."

"I don't know what to do," he said dismally.

"Sure you do, Father. We find a way to move our equipment to a town, right, Jessica? Patch up as best we can and sail into St. Louis," Melinda said.

"Well . . ." The professor suddenly grinned. He scratched his head as he looked at the tangled, broken mess on the beach—the confusion which had been his airship. "We did it before, didn't we?"

"That's right! We did it before."

"Cadge?" Jessica called Dana to her. "Ki and I are going to walk out, try to find a road and follow it to somewhere where there is a wagon for hire."

"All right. I take it you want me to stay here and watch things."

"No, we want you to come along and bring the wagon back."

"Bring it back— That won't take three of us, Jessie."

"No, it won't. Ki and I are going on ahead to St. Louis."

"To St. Louis? Why?" Cadge asked, his brow furrowing.

"You know darn well, Mister. Gregor is going to be heading that way with all possible speed. We intend to stop him."

"You're going after Schultz."

"Given the opportunity, yes."

"That's my job, Jessica," Cadge Dana said quietly.

"Is it? How do you intend to arrest anyone in Missouri,

156

Cadge? You have a warrant or something?"

"Jessica . . . how in hell do *you* intend to do that?"

Jessie looked at Ki and then back at Cadge. "We don't, Cadge. We mean to stop them, that's all. Gregor's got enough opium to ruin hundreds of lives. He's a killer. Ki and I aren't worried about warrants and other legal niceties at this point. But it's not something a lawman should be involved in."

"Or a reporter."

"Or a reporter— You're not a lawman at all, are you?"

Dana sighed. "Badges are easy to come by. I thought it might help somewhere along the line."

"It's not helping here. That's the plan. What do you say?"

"I have a hard time arguing with you, Jessica Starbuck. . . . All right, we'll do it your way. But—"

She put a finger to his lips, replaced it with her own lips and then turned to Ki. "It's all settled," the lady said.

Melinda asked, "What about Father and me?"

"There's plenty for you to do here." Sperry was already dismantling his burner. "Gregor went down on the far side of the river. I don't know where a ferry is, but I saw nothing near. He's not going to swim the river just to find you. The man is on his way to St. Louis. I know it."

Cadge Dana, Jessie, and Ki started out. They expected to find a wagon road running parallel to the river and did, not half a mile on. Hiking along it, they were overtaken by a wagon drawn by oxen. The driver was a German immigrant with a stubby pipe pushed into his whisker-wreathed mouth. He either didn't understand or pretended not to when they offered to hire his wagon.

Thumbing them toward the back of the wagon, empty now, but smelling strongly of manure, he said, "Ride."

They rode.

If the four-corners town they came to down the trail had a name they never learned it. There was no sign on the road, nothing on the buildings to identify the place.

They jumped from the back of the wagon as it rolled on through the town; the German again either did not know or care what they said when they asked him to stop.

"Well." Cadge stood nearly in the middle of the street as he spoke; there was no traffic. "They must at least have a stable, don't you think?"

"Somewhere." Jessica pointed toward a general store. "I wonder if they've got material in there, and kerosene?" There was only one way to find out and so they fanned out in all directions.

It was a suprisingly well stocked general store. Jessie found silk at a reasonable price, though the clerk blinked when she asked for four bolts. Rope was plentiful. Although Dana never found a livery stable he found a wagon to rent, and Ki, talking to people up and down the street, came up with a team of Missouri mules.

"Something's bound to go wrong," Cadge said pessimistically. "The way this trip has gone, nothing can be this easy."

Jessica laughed. "Cadge, every life, every endeavor has a turning point. We're right on the edge of success here. Don't be clouding up on us now."

"Habit," Cadge said, and it turned out that his foreboding was too accurate. They pulled the wagon to the back of the general store, rolled a barrel of kerosene down the plank ramp to the wagon, and stood it up.

Lashing the barrel down, Ki said, "That's it; you're set. The silk's up front."

Ki slapped the near mule on the flank and the team moved out smartly as Cadge lifted a hand. Still he looked worried— or maybe he was just disappointed to be out of the action now.

"You and me, alone again, Ki," Jessica said.

"It has never worked against us before. We have done much, you and I alone."

"The question is, what do we do now?" Jessica Starbuck asked, removing her flat-crowned hat to brush back her hair with her fingers before replacing it.

"Two horses. Find the nearest ferry. Track down Tyler Gregor. Eliminate this opium trade of Schultz's."

"How do you manage to make it all sound so simple?"

"I'm sure it won't be simple, Jessica," Ki answered. "But you asked me what must be done, and logically, that is the sequence."

"No time for sleep, for eating, for resting?"

"Those," Ki replied, "are *luxuries*, not what must be done, Jessica."

She smiled. Now and then Ki took her seriously when she was joking; this time he had fallen for it. Straight-faced, he looked across the dusty alley toward the forest, toward St. Louis far beyond.

"Horses," she said, taking his arm, squeezing it.

There was no livery stable, as they had already discovered, but Ki had made a few contacts already. The man who had rented him the mules was ready to sell socks, shoes, wife, and children after seeing the hard money Ki was carrying. Now as he stood against the bar in a saloon called "Everyman's Rest," drinking up what he could of the first windfall, he grinned as Ki and Jessica entered, looking for still more of a screwing.

"Damn outlanders," the man, whose name was Carroll French, muttered to his whiskered partner. "Hello there! Need more mules, my friend?"

"We are trying to hire two saddle horses," Ki said. "We want to ride through to St. Louis. The animals can be left there or we can hire someone to ride them back. If you know someone who wishes to sell outright, that will do as well."

"Reg?" Carroll French asked, rubbing his jaw. One of his glassy eyes winked at his sidekick.

"How much?" Reg asked.

"The going rate," Ki answered.

"Two good saddle ponies, tack included, hundred dollars each if you want to rent them, two hundred apiece to buy," Reg said. He expected to be bargained with, but in another minute he was sorry he hadn't asked double, triple that. The young lady with the—Indian, Chinaman, what was he?— began to stack up gold coins on the bar and the deal was struck before Reg could finish his tumbler of whiskey.

"Come on," was all he could say, scraping up the money, except for twenty dollars, which French had loaned him minutes before, and snatched up. "I'll show you where they are."

The horses were in fact his wife's property, a wedding gift from her Kentucky father, but Reg decided he had made the deal of his life. Besides, he wanted to keep drinking.

Both were grays, meant to be a team for his wife's surrey.

But the surrey had been sold one Christmas and the horses broken to saddle. Ki walked around them once. They were sound, and if the price was high, their immediate need made a few dollars unimportant.

"Y'all have a good journey," Reg said. They didn't answer except for Ki's nod, and Reg could only stand in the alley, tugging at his whiskers, wondering as the strange pair rode off out of the town. Shrugging, Reg counted his money and walked rather crookedly back into the saloon.

They ran into Tyler Gregor at the head of the alley.

It was so unexpected that Jessie and Ki both froze for one critical moment. In that moment Gregor's gunhands grabbed for their guns. On horseback, their bullets flew wild with the first volley, but Ki had no confidence that the bad marksmanship would continue.

He slapped Jessie's horse hard on the rump and it took off between two buildings, Jessica looking daggers at him as she tried to bring her Colt to bear.

Ki whipped a *shuriken* into the throat of a red-faced thug and saw it strike home, saw his horse rear up. A blast from a Winchester sent Ki to the side of his horse. Indian-style he sailed another *shuriken* up under the gray's neck. A hand flung up before his target's face saved the man's life, but the throwing star knifed through flesh and tendons and, holding a bloody hand, the man took to his heels, yelling with pain.

Guns were sighted at Ki, but the sudden emergence of a buckboard from an alleyway cut off the line of fire.

"Ned! Move it, out of the way!" Tyler Gregor shouted, but there was no way his man could hold up the team or turn it in those tight quarters.

The buckboard bounced over a deep rut and careened toward Ki. With the gray rearing, Ki lost his grip and, instead of flinging himself to the ground, he leaped from the stirrups toward the bed of the bouncing, out-of-control buckboard.

Ki's feet missed the wagon bed and hit the ground hard, but his hands kept their grip on the tailgate as the wagon bounced from side to side and rolled on through the mounted men.

Bullets splintered the bed of the wagon and urged the

already-panicked horses on into a flat-out run.

Leaning as it made the corner the buckboard exited the alley and careened onto the main road. The driver, a rat-faced man with a sallow complexion, stared back at Ki with wide eyes as the *te* master pulled himself up into the wagon bed and went for him.

Ki's hand latched onto the Gregor man's shirt collar, and he flung him from the wagon to roll through the dust to the side of the road.

Ki stepped into the box and reached for the trailing reins, bringing the horses under gradual control, yet not halting their run as they raced along the river road away from the little town.

Looking back, he saw no one, but Gregor was a very persistent man, as he well knew. From the ash and birch trees beside the road a rider emerged at a full gallop and Ki slowed the team, letting Jessica Starbuck catch up with him.

"I was ready to go back and get you out of there," she said as her gray horse pranced nervously. "And here you come in a buckboard!"

"You know what that is back there," Ki said, nodding toward the wagon bed.

Jessie hadn't seen it at first, but now she did. The burner from Gregor's balloon, all brass and steel, was strapped into the wagon bed beside a few bolts of new silk.

"Yes," she answered, "and I know what to do with it. I don't suppose the mail sack is back there too?"

"I didn't see it."

Ki was into the bed. He took the burner and overboarded it. A minute later he was using the simplest of man's tools to finish it forever. He hefted the rock and smashed the burner to useless junk. The silk he threw on the ground and set fire to. The horses were unharnessed and Ki hurriedly mounted one, sending the other off into the woods.

Then Gregor was behind them and St. Louis dead ahead. They had nothing to do but ride north and finish off this job. Or so they thought until the gunmen came toward them out of the deep woods.

Chapter 16

"Jessica!"

She hadn't seen the riders at first. Now she wheeled, drawing her .38 Colt, and shot the first man in the face, sending him somersaulting from the back of the roan he rode. Ki was on the ground again and the second Gregor hireling tried to ride him down.

Ki stepped to one side, grabbed the stirrups and heaved, and the gunman pitched from the saddle. On his knees as Ki came toward him, he tried to blast the *te* master with the rifle he held, but Ki's side-kick disarmed him, and a second kick nearly took his head off.

Flopping back, the man lay still, blood leaking from his nostrils and through broken teeth. Ki stood over him as Jessie rode up, holstering her pistol.

"Maybe we'd better ride. What are you looking at, Ki?"

"I never saw either of these two before."

"I've never even seen Tyler Gregor. So what?"

"They didn't follow us from the little town back there. They weren't in the fight I had in the alley—I'll bet on that."

"So Schultz knows already."

"Somehow," Ki answered, "Schultz knows."

There was no mystery to it. Starting on again, they spotted the telegraph line nearer to the river. Ki pointed it out and Jessica nodded.

He knew, all right. The drug king knew they were coming.

The great red-brick brewery was four stories high. Underneath it were caves used for storing beer at a constant cool temperaure. The place was well fenced and well guarded.

162

Jessica dragged into St. Louis at sundown, fighting a rush of homeward-bound workers and shoppers. Buggies clattered up the brick road before the brewery, which was silent, empty just now, the workday completed.

"Where to?" Ki asked.

"Bed," Jessica answered. The two-day ride had her exhausted. "My butt's out of practice."

"All right. Any particular place?"

"The Empress of Russia. The owner is Frank Bosworth. He knew Father, and well."

"Are you beginning to think we need help?" Ki asked.

"Aren't you? We've got a big man in this community to fight, Ki—employer of hundreds of people, bound to have political clout. Yes, we need help. We can't take him to court and win—I'd bet on that—and we can't simply eliminate him."

"And," Ki said, "he knows we're here."

"Something we'd better not forget. I just wonder *why,* Ki? Why is Schultz involved in this at all? He's got to have money, probably all he could ever need, from the looks of the brewery."

"Some men never get enough," Ki answered.

"Maybe Frank can give us some insight."

"We'll see. How far?"

Jessica looked around. She hadn't been in St. Louis in a long while. It had grown. There was a cop directing traffic at a corner—amazing. Wagons were backed up for two blocks. Jessica shouted her question at him. "Where's the Empress of Russia?"

"In Moscow," a stranger shouted back. The policeman just pointed, and they turned right onto a narrower, quieter street, which Jessica seemed to remember.

The street opened onto a vast circular courtyard paved with cinderblocks. A dozen full-grown elms grew in the tiny park in the middle of the courtyard. Ladies in silk, bustles wagging, hands tucked into fur muffs, moved along paved sidewalks.

The Empress of Russia was ornate, sporting six Doric columns across the front porch. A man in red livery stood by, top-hatted, awaiting fashionable guests.

He didn't alter his expression as the young, beautiful honey-blond woman in blue jeans and a man's checked cotton shirt swung down from the back of a weary gray horse, but his nose seemed to lift a little.

Ki and Jessie hitched their horses to the iron rail and walked up the broad steps.

"Have you the right address?" the doorman asked stiffly but with professional politeness.

"I want to see Mr. Bosworth. The name is Jessica Starbuck."

"I'll send a boy to see if Mr. Bosworth is in," the doorman answered, and after opening the door for three matrons with satin dresses and fantastic hats, he did just that.

The boy didn't return. Frank Bosworth himself appeared in minutes. "Jessica!" he said, coming out to take her hands. "Come in, come in, please!"

A fastidious little man with thin, plastered-down dark hair, Bosworth was beaming. If the people in the grand, chandelier-lit lobby turned to stare at Jessie and Ki, Bosworth himself was all warmth and friendship.

"My office is this way. The white door. What in the world are you doing here, Jessica? The last I heard you were in Dakota or California—one of those border states."

Jessica laughed. Frank Bosworth was an easterner who considered himself a pioneer by actually trekking—in a private Pullman—all the way to the Mississippi River.

Bosworth offered drinks, which Ki and Jessica refused, poured himself a large Scotch, and sat down at his leather-covered desk. "What can I do for you, Jessica? Or are you just here for a good dinner and a night's rest? Try the Peking duck . . . the squab is one of Andre's specialties too . . ."

Jessica leaned forward in her chair. "We've brought you a problem a little larger than that, I'm afraid, Frank."

"Oh?" Bosworth, who had been looking at his whiskey rather than actually drinking it, now took a sip. "And what is that, Jessica?"

"Do you know Gustav Schultz?" At Bosworth's nod, she told him what had happened and how Schultz was implicated.

"But—I know the man, Jessica! He's an outstanding citizen—my God, he's an Elk!"

"There's always a chance we could be wrong," Ki said.

"But you don't think so, obviously."

"No, we don't think so."

"Where does he live, Frank?" Jessica asked.

"You know, I feel like a traitor of some kind," Bosworth said unhappily. "I know Gustav very well indeed. Yet, I know you, Jessica, and I knew your father too well to think that you're coming to me with some imaginative tale. His house," the man went on with a sigh, "is in Green Gardens. I don't know the name of the street. It's the big white one on the hill. Anyone can point it out to you."

"What about the Chinese connection?" Ki asked.

"Gustav has been very active in the Chinese community," Bosworth said. "All of us have, but he especially. Trying to raise their living conditions, close down those despicable cribs—young girls of thirteen, fourteen, in virtual slavery. He's given many of them jobs at the brewery, and he has several Chinese house servants."

Jessica and Ki exchanged a glance. No matter what Bosworth thought he was telling them, he was simply confirming the fact that Gustav Schultz had deep connections with the Chinese community, the obvious market for imported opium.

"You will at least eat and take rooms—pardon me, " Bosworth said. "This thing has me upset."

"We will at least do that," Jessica answered, putting on her most gracious smile. "But I think we'd better eat in our rooms."

"Oh? Oh . . . I see." Bosworth frowned deeply. "You think some of these thugs followed you here?"

"I'm afraid there's always the chance."

"Yes. Well, if you don't want the marshal called in, I can at least post two of my security men near your rooms—just in case."

"That would be appreciated," Jessica said, rising. "Speaking for myself I need some sleep, and badly, just now."

Outside, as Bosworth went off to find his hotel security people, Ki said, "Four hours, Jessica?"

"That should be enough." It wouldn't be enough sleep at all, but she was damned if she was going to eat and sleep in luxury while this remained unresolved. It was time to drop the hammer on Gustav Schultz and drop it hard. "Four hours."

The lobby was a lot emptier when Ki and Jessica came down the curved staircase later that night, but there were enough people around to wonder what the Empress of Russia was coming to as they walked across the blue carpet toward the tall outer doors.

Their horses, by arrangement with Frank Bosworth, had been taken to a stable in exchange for two fresh mounts. These were standing in the alley next to the hotel, watched by yet another security guard.

"Have you seen anyone around?" Ki asked Bosworth's man.

"Just the usuals—our local drifters, cadgers. One Chinese fellow, seemed to be drunk or something."

"Thank you," Ki said. They swung aboard the horses and started out across the courtyard. Gaslights blossomed with fire around the ring of shops and hotels. In no time at all, St. Louis might even be civilized.

But it wasn't yet, not quite yet.

Their tail picked them up before they had even finished crossing the cinder-stone courtyard to enter the narrow alley opposite.

"Did you see him?" Jessica asked.

"The Chinese?" Ki answered. "Yes."

He wore a black silk costume, a red headband, and soft slippers. He was *tong*, and it was obvious to Ki if it wasn't to Jessica. They had problems larger than taking in one beer baron. Out West they had had a half-dozen Gregor men to deal with, but now they had entered a labyrinth of organized crime. The *tong* and their hatchet men, obviously on orders from Schultz, were determined to finish off these crazy interlopers.

Ki wondered how large a stranglehold Schultz had on St. Louis. Certainly he had an influence on the workings of the city that would have astonished most of St. Louis' citizens— and maybe even a few of the local authorities. Ki, with a knowledge of how these things worked, figured that dozens of

166

local politicians and officials had taken bribes to do this small thing or that, none of them knowing that they were being caught up in a vast web of vice and crime that they couldn't speak out against without being involved themselves.

It didn't take a lot of skill to lock up a city. Just a little patience—and a lot of money.

Green Gardens was beyond being exclusive. You had to have enough money to start your own bank to even think about living there. Huge homes, most in the antebellum style of the deep South, stood half hidden behind cypress and magnolia trees, at the end of long driveways of crushed brick. Lights blazed from the windows.

The beer king's house wasn't that hard to find. Using Bosworth's description they located the three-story white house on top of the hill. A wrought-iron fence encircled grounds covering many acres. Vines crept up the fence, and armed guards walked their patrols behind it.

They passed by and halted their horses finally a quarter of a mile up the road beneath the dark elm trees. Ki said, "I guess I'll go in and take a look around."

"You guess what? Ki, that's not the way to do it."

"I think it is," he replied.

"Then I'm going with you, my friend."

Ki shook his head. "I don't think you would pass at all."

"Pass?"

"As an Oriental. Most whites can't tell the difference between a Chinese and a Korean."

"Or a Japanese," Jessica said, getting his drift. "But Ki, you cannot just simply walk up to the gate, present yourself, and go in."

"Why?" Ki asked. He was smiling.

"You're serious, aren't you?"

"Quite serious. I'm going in, and if I can I'm coming back out with Gustav in tow."

"While I do what?"

"I thought perhaps you might speak to Bosworth again and find out if there are any local authorities above reproach, so that if Gustav Schultz is brought in—"

"Federal marshals," Jessica said.

"You *would* think of that," Ki replied. "Seriously, there must be someone above reproach in this town. You can ask Bosworth."

"And that will get me well out of the way of any fighting, won't it, Ki?"

"Jessica Starbuck, have I ever tried to steer you away from the fighting?" Ki asked with a straight face.

"Most of the time. Hasn't worked well, has it?" She was momentarily serious, touching his shoulder with concern. "If you think it might work, go ahead. But damn it all, Ki, you watch yourself!"

Ki waited until Jessica had turned her horse and started away before he slipped from the saddle, looped the reins to his pony around the elm branch, and, hunching his shoulders, started shuffling back toward the iron gate to Gustav Schultz's house.

Chapter 17

"Dawg" FitzGerald looked up after lighting his freshly-rolled cigarette to see the hunched Oriental shuffling toward the gate on slightly bowed legs, his hands folded together. What in Jesus' name was going on? There had been a procession of messengers, Chinese gang lords, and politicians through the gate all night. The boss had something big up his sleeve—or he had big trouble.

Dawg, with his smoke fixed between his lips, walked toward the gate, shotgun in his hands. He didn't recognize this one, but then the Chinese had been sending around a lot of runners tonight.

"Good evening, please," Ki said, bowing low to conceal his face. "This is urgent for Mr. Schultz."

Dawg FitzGerald frowned briefly. They never asked for the boss by his right name. It was always "the Master," just to keep them out of the habit of even thinking that name.

Yet all day people had been coming with urgent messages of one sort or another, and some of them didn't even seem to know what they were doing, or who in hell they wanted to talk to. This one at least knew that much.

Dawg leaned close to the locked iron gate and said, "Okay. Got your card?"

Ki's heart did a little skip. *The card*. Of course, there would be some kind of identification needed. Why hadn't he simply gone over the fence in a dark corner? Because that wouldn't assure the access to the house that a guarded escort did. That was his thinking originally. Wrong guess.

"Please?" Ki said humbly, bowing again.

Dawg sighed and said, "Your card, my friend."

Ki's hand shot through the iron gate and grabbed Dawg's collar. Yanking back hard, he slammed the guard's head against the iron bars and Dawg slumped into a nice quiet little nap.

Ki searched the man through the gate, his eyes darting to the darker recesses of the yard. He came up with an iron keyring. Ki found the key he wanted on the fourth try. He eased on through, leaving the gate unlocked.

After dragging Dawg back into the shrubbery, he searched him more thoroughly, finding a common playing card—the ace of hearts. There was no reason for the man to be carrying a single card that Ki could think of unless it was some sort of identification, and so he pocketed it. He also took Dawg's .44 Remington revolver, hardly one of Ki's favorite weapons— too messy, too noisy, unnecessary, but perhaps on this night useful.

The great front double doors were dark. Ki walked directly to them, figuring he was safer that way than snooping around for a side exit or an open window.

He rapped three times and the door opened. A short Chinese man with pouched eyes, dressed in the black silk of the *tong*, stood there. Ki handed him the playing card and bowed.

The Chinese closed the door behind him and left Ki standing in a vaulted foyer cluttered with Oriental artifacts, much jade and ivory, a few tapestries.

The Chinese returned after fifteen minutes, bowed to Ki, and gestured with his head. Ki followed him into the interior of the house. Up a back staircase they ascended to the second floor of the mansion. Ki followed his guide down a darkened corridor to a small room with a wire-mesh window set into it. The Chinese knocked, and Ki entered.

Behind the carved mahogany desk a huge, big-bellied man wearing a blue polished-cotton vest beneath his dark coat sat cleaning his fingernails with a gold knife.

Schultz. At last.

"Yes?" Sleepy eyes lifted to Ki.

"I have a message from Gregor," Ki said, bowing low, keeping his body curled, hopefully appearing shrunken.

"Have you?" Schultz asked disinterestedly. "And what is it, *Ki?*"

Ki leaped forward, but he was too late. The shadow moving against the wall was cast by a thick Chinese with a heavy club. The club thudded against Ki's skull behind the ear, putting out the lights. He clawed at the edge of Schultz's desk, saw the fat man smirk. Then he was hit again, and the darkness became final.

The room had that peculiar dusty scent of potatoes, and when Ki managed to claw his eyes open, he saw why. He was leaning against a burlap sack filled with potatoes, surrounded by other sacks.

A light burned low somewhere and by it he could see other goods, vast quantities of them, hanging hams, flour, corn, and tinned fruit. Gustav Schultz seemed determined never to go hungry.

Ki tried to rise and on the second attempt he made it to his feet. He walked in a slow circle around the windowless room. Pipes overhead, that single locked door, solid stone floor, dripping water, potatoes. He sat down again rubbing his head behind his ear, automatically patting his pockets for his *shuriken*.

Gone. As was the gun. Ki had expected nothing else.

A second, closer inspection of the room brought no further results. He was locked in, trapped until Schultz decided what to do with him. And it didn't seem Schultz had many options. Ki sat, watching the door like a caged big cat.

Bypassing Bosworth, Jessica went straight to the United States Marshal's office on Gower Street. She waited twenty minutes before a harried looking man with a hawk nose and dark eyes entered. He looked at her, seemingly perplexed, glanced at the wall clock and went into his office. The male secretary who had let Jessie in at this late hour shrugged and got back to reading his *Police Gazette*.

"Wasn't that the marshal?" Jessie asked.

The secretary had to pull his eyes away from some seductive tale of a double decapitation. "Yes, Miss. Marshal Drew."

"Can he see me now? It's urgent."

"He hasn't told me."

Frustrated, Jessica suggested tautly, "Perhaps you could ask him?"

"It's late, Miss."

"It can't wait until tomorrow, I'm sorry. Since the marshal is in now, I would like to see him," she said, spacing her words out so that each one was a demand of its own.

"Yes," the secretary said as if humoring a madwoman, "I'll see." He rose, tapped at the half-glassed door and went in, leaving Jessica temporarily alone. She glanced at the two decapitated bodies the artist had imagined and turned to lean against the desk, arms folded.

The secretary came back out shaking his head. "Have to be tomorrow, Miss," he said.

"Turn around," Jessica said sharply, and the secretary, stunned at the gun in this beautiful woman's hand, did so automatically, his hands going into the air. "March back in there and tell him this concerns several murders and the interstate trafficking of drugs."

Unhappily the secretary did so, and when he emerged this time he left the door to the office open. "Marshal Drew will see you, Miss."

"Thank you," Jessica said with a smile. She holstered her pistol unobtrusively and entered the office. The hawk-nosed man had a stack of papers, a pistol, and a bottle of whisky on his desk. He looked tired, and had the essentially wary look of peace officers everywhere.

"Guess you wanted to see me tonight," he said drily.

"I did."

He glanced at her pistol and nodded, pouring a glass of whisky as he leaned back. "Mike says you got a big story to tell."

"Big enough."

"Murder and drugs?" The marshal slugged his whisky down.

"For beginners."

"Then you'd better tell me all about it, lady. Don't mind this," he said, meaning the whisky. "I was supposed to be off duty three hours ago; it's just hard to get off duty in this damned town. I can still listen and think—and if necessary," he said, looking at his sidearm, "shoot."

Jessica laid it out for him, and Drew, at first simply patient, became interested, and then intent. He had time to drink another glass of Kentucky whisky before she was finally through.

"Gustav Schultz?" the marshal asked incredulously.

"Almost certainly, yes."

"And your friend is out there alone? He must be some kind of man if he suspects all of this and went in there anyway. Listen. If I can get the judge to write me some warrants we'll have a look."

"Is it necessary? Is there time? Ki is there alone. Perhaps you could just make a friendly call on Mr. Schultz."

"I don't know about that." The marshal was silent for a moment, drumming his fingers on his desk. "But it would keep me clear, just in case . . ."

"Just in case what?"

"In case," he said, rising, putting his own gun away, "a certain lady has a little too much imagination. Come on. I'm willing to have a look, and damned if I don't tend to believe you. Let's get on out there before any more murder's done."

The marshal was a slow-moving man, but he got his coat on in less than five minutes. He looked longingly at his bottle but put it away, turned off his lamp, and led Jessica out of the office. The secretary was gone now so the marshal locked the outer door, using up another entire minute figuring out how to do it. Jessie could only hope he was more efficient as a lawman.

They rode toward the Schultz house under a starry sky. The wind off the Mississippi was warm and moist. Unconsciously Jessie glanced skyward, searching for an aircraft. Funny, she thought, how an experience like hers could alter patterns of thought.

"No sense monkeying around," Drew told her. "Right up to the front gate and let's see what's happening."

They did that. Behind the gate a man with a white bandage on his forehead stood smoking sullenly. "That you, Dawg?" the marshal called out.

173

"Yeah." A shotgun appeared. "Who in hell's that?" the guard called back from the darkness.

"Marshal Drew."

"What do you want?" Dawg FitzGerald demanded.

"I want to see Mr. Schultz, Dawg. What else would I come out here for?"

"Maybe he don't wanta see you."

"Maybe he's going to have to," Drew said, flashing his badge. "You forget I carry this?"

"Shit. Come on ahead then," Dawg said, swinging the gate open. "I'll likely catch hell for this."

"Catch more if you try keeping me out," Drew promised him.

Together Drew and Jessica rode to the front of the house and swung down. Leading the way up the steps, the marshal banged on the door until a Chinese houseboy appeared.

"Schultz here? Marshal Drew."

"I see, I see," the Chinese said, bowing.

"If you have to see, that means he's here," Drew said, stepping across the threshhold. "In his office?"

Drew never stopped walking. The Chinese houseboy spouted off angrily in his own tongue as the marshal walked across the carpeted floor to a staircase and climbed to the second floor, the effort seeming to tire him. At a white door, Drew rapped once and pushed on through to a book-lined office where a fat man sat behind his desk.

"What is this?" Gustav Schultz demanded angrily.

"Christ," Drew answered, wiping at his nose, "you're gettin' old and careless, Gus. Here's another one knows what you been up to." The marshal turned, cocked gun in his hand. He put the muzzle to Jessica's temple and ordered, "Hand over that fancy pistol of yours, lady, will you please."

Jessica, her heart dropping, complied. Schultz looked vastly annoyed, Drew simply sleepy. The marshal said, "I guess you can handle it from here on. Gus, I'm about to get tired of this shit. I'll expect a bonus."

Then the marshal was gone and Jessica Starbuck was left to stand facing the opium king.

Ki was behind the door, body tensed, the muscles of his

174

body poised like steel springs when he heard the key in the lock. He had planned his first move already and he had nearly struck his blow when the too-familiar lady was pushed into the room. The door locked behind her.

"Jessica!"

She sat on the floor looking up at Ki with bemusement. She just shook her head, thrust out her hand, and let Ki tug her to her feet.

"I blew it," she said.

"Apparently," Ki admitted, looking around the storeroom. "So did I, Jessica."

"No way out, I take it." Or Ki wouldn't have been there. Still, rising, dusting off, she performed the essentially useless circuit of the room.

"None."

"What's the plan, Ki?" Jessie asked, sagging onto a sack of potatoes next to Ki. He smiled and briefly she rested her head against his shoulder.

There was no plan, could be no plan. They had finally run out of luck, it seemed. The cavalry wasn't going to arrive, no one was going to toss a gun in the window, since there was none. Lightning wasn't going to strike the sinner Gustav Schultz and make a saint of him.

What was going to happen was they were going to sit there and wait until Schultz had figured out exactly *how* he was going to do what he had to do.

Kill Jessie and Ki.

Chapter 18

"You—get up! Up, up!"

The Chinese was emphatic about it. He had five more men in black, hatchets in their hands, behind him. Jessica stretched and looked at Ki.

"I guess he means us."

Any idea Ki had had about fighting his way out of there was crushed by the presence of Jessica Starbuck and the number of the enemy. The *tong* men were flat-faced, cruel-eyed. They made their living chopping up people who didn't care to go along with the *tong* leaders. There would be no hesitation to kill.

Ki rose as well. His mouth was dry, the pulse at his temple pounding. He had to fight back the instinct to go for the leader's throat. Still, they were going to die, there was no doubt in Ki's mind about it. Why not try it?

But he held back. Maybe there was another chance, a last chance ahead of them. *"Te,"* he heard one of the Chinese mutter as he nodded at Ki, and he knew that they would not underestimate him, not these hatchet men.

They were taken out into the stone-floored corridor and led toward a back door where another black-clad, scarlet-sashed Chinese stood, arms folded, watching.

The door was opened and all hell broke loose. Ki reacted instantly, throwing Jessica to one side, diving that way himself as the shotgun cut down the screaming, fleeing Chinese thugs. Even so Ki took a pellet in the arm. For the moment that didn't matter.

Three Chinese were down, one still alive and writhing, and Ki grabbed for his hatchet.

"Damn it!" he yelled over his shoulder. "Let's get after them."

"I got you, didn't I?" Cadge Dana said, reloading his scatter gun.

"A pellet, maybe two. Don't worry about it. Let's get after them."

"Cadge?" Jessie rose shakily to her feet. Ki had already started running up the corridor back into the house and they started after him, Dana handing Jessie a big blue .44 Colt revolver. "How did you know? Why aren't you back with Sperry and Melinda?"

"They didn't need me. And you weren't hard to find. Knowing you two, you'd come right after Schultz."

There wasn't time for any further conversation. From ahead of them somewhere a rifle barked, its report thundering through the hall.

It was Ki who had drawn the fire. Hoping to stop the hatchet men before they could reorganize, he had been hot on their heels. One of the Chinese had foolishly turned to challenge the *te* master, and Ki, on the run, had flipped the hatchet he carried into the center of the thug's chest, stopping his heart as he flopped back.

Ki picked up the *tong* member's hatchet and ran on. It was Schultz he wanted. His theory was that of most fighting men: Cut off the head of the beast and the body will die.

Too anxiously he raced up the stairs toward the beer baron's office, and nearly ran into a bullet fired by Dawg FitzGerald, who had rushed into the house at Cadge's shot.

Ki dove for the floor, but simultaneously flipped his hatchet up and into Dawg's body. It caught the hired gun in the groin, lengthening his legs by an inch or two, and Dawg dropped his rifle to reel back, screaming like a woman, the ax handle protruding from his crotch.

Ki had no time for sympathy. He leaped at Dawg as the gunman fell to the floor, picked up the neglected Winchester, and kicked in Gus Schultz's office door.

The big man was gone.

Ki crossed the room and found the throw rug—Chinese, five hundred years old—thrown to one side. The trap door

177

was where the rug used to be.

He spun as someone burst in the room. He dropped to one knee to lever a cartridge into the breech of the repeating rifle.

Jessica came up short and lifted a hand as Cadge stormed in behind her.

"Not here?"

"There," Ki said, nodding toward the trap door. "It might stir up something to open it."

Cadge Dana was more impulsive. "That's the only way to catch the son of a bitch." He flipped the trap door back, and a firestorm of bullets whined upwards, ripping at the plastered ceiling, putting the green-glass lantern out. Cadge had had enough, and didn't seem to care what happened to him now. With one hand he shoved the shotgun he carried into the trap and pulled the trigger.

Thunder roared through the room. Rising black powder-smoke filled the office of the brewer. Someone below yelled out with terrible pain. Cadge, reloading quickly, snapped the shotgun shut and stood over the escape hatch, firing into it again.

The smoke was thick enough now to obscure their vision, to sting nostrils and eyes. Cadge dropped into the trap door, neglecting the ladder in his haste. Ki and Jessie were close behind.

Dana hit the floor far below hard and got up hobbling, cursing. Ki, sliding and skidding, but using the ladder, came down more safely. Jessica was right behind them. Cadge, limping, moved toward a closed and barred wooden door and beat futilely at it. Before Ki could reach it to help, Dana blew the door open with another load of buckshot.

Jessie and Ki exchanged a glance. Dana was like a man possessed, and it was hard to figure him either for a lawman or enraged newsman caught up in events. He was reckless to the point of being suicidal.

They couldn't slow Dana down. He hurled himself through the door into the yard beyond, and rifles opened up, spitting flame and lead at him.

Ki, moving to the side, rolled into the yard, came up with his Winchester ready, and levered through six rounds as fast as

178

he could work the lever. Jessie fired from the doorway, beating the ambushers back.

The hired thugs broke and ran, sprinting toward the iron fence beyond the trees. Cadge was on their heels, stopping to fire a shot or two, racing after them to reduce the range, firing again. He picked one man off the fence, and then another. They fell into the shrubbery and lay still.

Those who made it across the fence had mounted concealed horses and were racing hell for it by the time Jessie and Ki caught up to add their following fire to Dana's.

"Come on!" Dana shouted, leaping for the fence. Ki put a hand on Dana's shoulder and gently pulled him back to the grass.

"Wait a minute."

"He'll get away, dammit, Ki!"

"I don't think so," Ki answered.

"Dammit, he can't get away—I won't allow it!"

"He won't. I think it's time you told us now, Cadge, don't you?" Ki asked gently.

"I've been on his trail for a long while," Cadge said at last. "That's why I took that job as a newsman, why I wanted to come to St. Louis."

"I don't understand," Jessica said.

"His name isn't Schultz," Dana said with an impatient sigh. "At least at one time he called himself by another name —Bull Calahan, if it's important."

"He was in San Francisco?"

"Sure. That was where he began. Running slave girls, trading in opium. He poisoned people, Jessie, Ki, took their lives away from them. People were chopped up for dog meat if they got in Calahan's way.

"Young women . . ."

"What happened, Dana?" Ki asked.

"My wife," he said, "was Chinese. Kidnapped, drugged— I don't know what went on, but they found her one day in an alley. Calahan was already gone by then, but everyone knew he was behind it. The thing was, the San Francisco police didn't much care as long as the victims were Chinese."

"You cared."

"I looked up every alley in San Francisco for Calahan. Finally I realized he had left the city, but I had no idea where, until one of my informants told me about a load of opium coming in to be delivered to St. Louis.

"I started looking at Gustav Schultz's past—it doesn't go back very far. He's Calahan. I'll kill him, I swear it. If you hadn't let him get away, Ki . . ."

"I told you," Ki answered. "He didn't get away."

"Damn sure of it, aren't you?" Dana said hotly. He stood reloading his shotgun with trembling fingers.

"Yes, I am. It would be beyond logic," Ki said. "You saw the men run away, vault the fence, take to horseback. I saw Gustav Schultz today, Cadge. The man weighs three hundred pounds! Do you really think he sprinted over here and climbed the fence?"

Cadge shifted his gaze back to the house. "He let us find the trap door."

"Sure. It didn't matter what happened to a few hired thugs. He wanted us to think he escaped, but he didn't. He never had time."

"He's still inside, then."

"I think so. Cadge—promise me you won't kill him if we do find Schultz."

"Ki, that's why I'm here!"

"Give me your promise, please." Ki's expression was hard now. Dana stared at him, knowing that Ki was a half-second away from taking Cadge out if he didn't make that promise.

"All right," he said with deep disgust. "You better have your reasons, Ki."

"I have my reasons," the *te* master answered.

They started back across the yard, still smelling gunsmoke. In the distance a police bell was clanging. There wasn't a firefight every evening at Green Gardens. Someone had gotten the local police. That didn't leave Ki and Jessie much time to finish up.

"Cadge, bring our horses around, will you? If you can find a buggy, that would be useful."

Dana was incensed. "What in bloody hell are you talking about, Ki! I came to fight, not to be somebody's goddamn stableboy."

180

Jessica put her hand on Cadge's arm. "Please, Cadge. Believe me, if Ki has a plan, it's best to follow it. He knows what he's doing. Haven't you done your share of fighting for now?"

Cadge looked at her for a long minute and then just spun away angrily, walking, shoulders hunched, toward the street. Ki said, "Let's go, Jessie. There may not be much time."

They reentered the ground floor hiding space and climbed the ladder to Schultz's office, Ki emerging first, moving cautiously to one side, ready for more warfare; but the room was silent. He looked into the hallway and stood listening for a long while. No one seemed to be in the house. There was no reason why any of Schultz's soldiers should have remained— except the dead ones.

"Well?" Jessica asked, looking around as Ki turned up the lamp in the corner behind Schultz's desk.

Ki seemed to know just what he was doing, although Jessica decided it couldn't have more than a hunch that turned out right. The samurai walked to the closet door behind the desk and swung it open.

There stood Gustav Schultz—or Bull Calahan—sweat raining off of him, his face ashen, his pink hands lifted.

"Don't kill me—I can pay you!"

"Fine," Ki said, "pay us."

Schultz blinked. "Is that all this is?" He grew a little more confident. "A shakedown? You went to extraordinary lengths, young man, young lady."

Jessica had been poking around. Now she said, "Here it is, Ki." It's not that easy to hide a wall safe, and this one was behind an Oriental hanging.

"Over there and open it quickly," Ki said.

"There's nothing much in there," Schultz bluffed. Ki pinched down on his neck, and excruciating pain shot through Schultz's skull.

"Open it, please. We don't have much time."

"All right! All right," the sweating fat man panted. He fumbled with the lock for longer than he should have but finally got it open. There was a row of neat stacks of currency in there, a bank bag, a small black book. Ki took the bank bag and filled it.

"You don't need that book. What do you need that for?" Schultz asked excitedly. "Take the money and go, take it!"

Ki thumbed through the coded book and tucked it into the sack as well. "All right," he said. "Now we can go."

"We? What do you want me for?" Schultz asked, backing away. He backed right into Jessie's cocked .38 and decided to go the other way without asking any more questions.

They went down the stairway, Schultz turning his head away from the not-so-pretty sight of Dawg FitzGerald. They crossed the foyer, Ki with the bag in his hand leading the way, Schultz with Jessica Starbuck's gun in his back, following.

The door opened just as they reached it and there stood Tyler Gregor, mail sack in his hands. "What the hell . . .!" he shouted. Then he threw the mailsack at Ki and ducked, coming up with his revolver. Jessica was first.

Stepping from behind Schultz she fired three times. Gregor went to his tiptoes, half turned, and slammed against the wall, blood smearing the beautiful mahogany paneling behind him as he slid to the floor.

The police bells were much nearer. "Hurry it up!" Jessica hissed. Schultz stepped daintily over his henchman, his eyes wide with horror. Ki shouldered the mail sack and caught up with them at the gate where Cadge Dana nervously looked across his shoulder and held up the buggy and team he had brought around.

His face froze as he saw Schultz—froze and then softened as he looked away, muttering, "Cops are right behind us."

Ki tossed the sack into the buggy and half dragged Schultz in behind him. Jessica leaped in beside Cadge as he whipped the horses forward.

"Are you giving him to me?" Cadge asked.

"No."

"I don't get it then—why not leave him for the police?"

"It might be a little difficult to explain all the bodies," Jessie pointed out.

"Here, turn up here," Ki said, pointing out a country road lined with trees. Cadge did so without comment, and an hour on they came to an old barn, where they pulled up and stepped down.

The barn, abandoned, still had a lantern on the wall, and Ki lit it as they went inside, closing the double doors behind them.

"Look here—" Schultz began, trying to recapture some indignation.

"Sit down," Cadge growled.

"Where?" the opium smuggler asked, looking around.

"There," Dana said, pushing him to the ground. "Sit there and shut your mouth, *Calahan*." The man called Schultz went paler yet, but he was quiet as Ki opened up Gregor's mailsack and started dumping out the oilskin-wrapped packages of opium.

"Your mail, it seems, has been delivered," Ki said, crouching over it.

"I don't know..." Schultz started to deny it all, but he couldn't come up with a lie even he could pretend to believe in.

Setting the mailsack aside for the time being, Ki opened the little bank bag and dumped the money and bonds it contained out on the ground. "There's nearly a quarter of a million there," Schultz said. "Take it. Go, before the police find you."

Ki ignored the man. Counting out some of the money, he piled the remainder into a stack and fished for a match. "What are you doing?" Schultz screamed. He tried to dive for Ki, but Cadge pushed him back to the ground.

Ki got his fire going easily. Money burns well, and in no time the stack was nothing but blackened paper, curled and useless.

"Mad," Schultz said, burying his face in his hands, "you're all mad."

It was the little black book that most interested Ki and Jessica. "Give me enough time," she said, "and I'll break the code. It can't be too complicated or it wouldn't work. To the right people this would be very interesting."

"It's only a record of my business transactions," Schultz protested.

"Yes," Jessica answered, "we know, and knowing what your business interests are, it's enough to hang you."

183

The night had grown cooler, but Schultz was sweating more profusely than ever. "There must be some way we can work things out," he said desperately.

"Maybe," Jessica said. "If you'll do a little something for us."

"You'd give me back the book?" Schultz asked, hopeful for the first time in hours.

"If you'll carry through with another bargain you made, yes."

"*Anything*, I'll do anything!"

Ki was listening but he was busy refilling the mail sack with its drug packets. Neither Cadge nor Ki interrupted Jessica. Schultz thought he had never seen such cold-eyed men as these two, not even among his own violent forces.

"What are you doing now?" he asked as Ki took the mail sack and went out. There was no answer. Schultz watched the door until Ki returned ten minutes later. "What did you do? Tell me!"

"Old well out there," Ki said quietly. "Dumped the stuff in it."

Schultz groaned and sat holding his head. It was a long night, but just before sunset they got Schultz to his feet and led him out into the coolness to clamber aboard the buggy.

"Where are we going? We had a deal!"

Again no one spoke to him. Cadge took the buggy to a low, grassy knoll, and they climbed out to stand looking southward as the sun rose. "Here it comes," Jessica said at last, and then they all saw it, drifting slowly toward them, a crimson balloon against the pale sky. "They made it."

"What's the matter with the three of you?" Schultz asked, looking from one face to the others. "Are you all crazy? What does the balloon matter now?"

"It matters," Jessica said, "to the old man who set out to do something impossible and succeeded. You owe him fifty thousand dollars, or will when he gives you your mail, and you're going to pay him—happily. Ki's counted out the money."

"You can't be serious. This! This is our bargain?" Schultz asked. Then he began laughing wildly. "Sure, sure, of course I'll pay the old man. Why not?"

184

They tracked the balloon's course in their buggy and were there when it finally set down not far from the town square. Ki and Cadge stood with Schultz while Jessica went off on some errand or other.

It was half an hour before a beaming Sperry climbed from the gondola, walked to Schultz, and said proudly, "Sir, your mail from San Francisco."

Schultz took the sack while the people around cheered. "And, sir," Schultz said, smiling broadly, "I am proud to present you with the prize money I promised. Good luck in future endeavors."

"Ki?" Jessica was back with Frank Bosworth, two uniformed policemen, and a man Ki didn't recognize. Jessie said to Schultz, "You know the district attorney, don't you, Mr. Schultz?"

Schultz's face collapsed. He started struggling and cursing, his eyes bulging out of his head. "We had a *deal*, we had a deal, you lying bitch!"

Jessica Starbuck shrugged. "Hell—I lied."

With a policeman on each arm, Schultz was dragged away, the district attorney, the black book in his pocket, following. Sperry, a bundle of money in his hand, look confused. Melinda held Ki's arm as the crowd, looking the balloon over, moved around them.

"There's your story, Cadge," Jessica said. "Last chapter."

"Thanks, Jessie. Thanks for not letting me kill the man, as much as he needed killing."

"Jessica?" Ki called over the crowd. "Empress of Russia?"

"Yes!" she shouted back. "Squab. Peas. Leek soup. And *sleep!*"

Cadge turned to her and asked, "And me?"

"What do you think?" Jessica asked. Hooking her arm around his she led him across the crowded square, never once looking back at the great crimson balloon.